The Cursed and The Dead: Silver and Lead

Avi Llio

Ixtab

Media

This book contains scenes that may be considered graphic or cruel.

For my family.
Working my way back to you.

The Cursed and The Dead:

Silver and Lead

Aces

See the town of Genesis. It sits waiting in an unending sea of bleached white sand. Few know it exists, and nobody finds it by accident. To stumble into such a desolate town is to find one last chance at salvation.

The surrounding expanse has been dead for millennia. Even death itself has forgotten about the town, and it could survive out of ignorance alone.

The town's buildings rest abandoned, little more than monuments to the futility of hope. Speculators who expected big returns for their investment had built the houses. Oil, trade, wayward travellers. They were right to suspect the town was important. It was destined for one great and dreadful act.

Only one resident remained. He called himself the mayor. He whittled away his dwindling years inside the Bad Moon Saloon, where he would drink and snore and drive himself half-mad with loneliness. On rare occasions, an unfortunate soul would stumble into town, and he would keep them company until they could leave with the monthly supply wagon.

His last day in Genesis was such a day. Not one but four men shambled into town in search of refuge. From his position behind the bar, he watched the four men play poker. Whether they had been there an afternoon or a week, none could tell you.

Consider the dramatis personae:

John, the first to enter. He arrived black clad and near feral, soused even before he reached for the whiskey. He had ridden his horse to death, he said, and he'd had half the mind to follow it.

To John's right sat Milton. He was a mountain of a man clad in wolf and bear furs. That his pride had forbidden him from removing these clothes and his constitution had landed him in a town such as Genesis was testament to his hardiness. Milton claimed to be trekking the entire country and nobody had the mind to contradict him.

Next to Milton sat Joshua, a travelling salesman whose goods perished out there in the wilderness. He was more accustomed to the ease and luxury of city life if his clothing and scrunched up nose were anything to go on. His hands toyed with the torn fabrics of his expensive suit.

Last was the scarred and placid Alfredo, donned in all white. He sat facing the door with one hand on his cards and the other never too far from his holster. It was Alfredo who had suggested the card game and Alfredo alone who offered no reason for being in such a place.

"Well?" said John.

Joshua looked at the pot, then at his cards. The lines in his face folded in on themselves for a second, and then he tossed in his hand. Milton thumbed his checks, cut them twice, and then folded. Only Alfredo remained. He looked down at his cards, at John, at the pile of checks and crumpled bills on the table, and smiled.

"I don't think you got shit," he said.

"Then bet. Quit wasting my time."

Alfredo laughed. "All we got is time out here, friend. Who knows when we'll get to leave?"

Milton grunted in agreement. "And who's saying we ever will?"

"Yes, one wonders," Joshua added.

"Oh, does one?" John said. "Look, you fellers ain't even in this hand no more, so how's about you both shut the hell up so we can play?"

Milton rolled his hands into fists for all of a half second before his body loosened and he closed his eyes. Joshua watched him and nodded.

"Something funny?" John said.

"Oh, no," replied Joshua, "Not at all. Just surprised it took this long for tempers to rise."

"Ain't no tempers raising here, and neither is this pendejo by the looks of it. Are you in or out, bud?"

Alfredo licked his thumb. "You keep talking, but you're saying nothing. No one here's intimidated by you."

"So do something!"

"Oh, I will."

A hostility lingered in the air as the two men sat frozen in their own bravado. It was only when Joshua slapped the table the spell broke and the two strangers returned to their cards. His voice rattled like a rusty cage as he tried to appeal to the table. "Gentlemen, please. We're not even playing big stakes here. Let's take a moment, hm? Relax, yes? Please? We're all stuck here in this purgatory—no offense, barkeep—so we may as well make the most of it."

Milton stood and spoke. His voice was as deep as he was tall. "Yeah, I gotta agree. John, buddy, you're getting awfully worked up over a fifty cents pot."

Alfredo spat out a single laugh. "Oh, shit, you're right, that is fifty cents. Ha. I guess I call then."

John shook his tired head and scraped his stubble with his thumb. "Of all the… Fine. Show 'em."

Alfredo did. Two pair. John grinned and lay down the same hand, except his came with an ace kicker. He dragged his paltry winnings toward him, then raked in the cards and washed them. Then he turned to Joshua and said, "What's all this about relaxing, then?"

"Ah," said Joshua. He waved at the mayor to prepare a fresh round of liquor. The four of them looked at their drinks with lascivious glee. "Well, we've got time to kill by my estimate, and perhaps we all have a tale or two up our sleeves. Four men, alone in the desert. We must have all had a few adventures to get here. How's about we all get to know each other? Lighten the mood, you know?"

"I'm not having no strangers know my past," said Alfredo.

"That's more than fine, my friends. In fact, perhaps we can avoid tales of our own transgressions for a time and focus on something else."

"What the hell are you talking about, pal?" Milton said.

"I mean, we've all heard storied, yes? Weird ones, big ones, you know. Surely you've all heard something on your travels. What's the strangest thing you've ever heard?"

"Oh, yeah, I gotcha now. Sure, I got plenty of those I don't mind sharing."

Alfredo took the deck from John and cut it. "I guess I heard a few things."

John sighed and looked down at the table. "How strange are we talking here?"

"Anything, really. Larger than life people, odd events. Interesting things."

"Ah. I see. Then you should know I've got you all licked as far as that goes."

"Yeah?" said Milton. "How about you start us off?"

Sundown Town

"You ever hear about the man they call the Wandering Lawmaker?
He was a kind of legend where I grew up. 'Course, this story happened elsewhere.
A ghost town named Reckoning."
"You reckon?"
"Clever. Do you want to hear this or not?"

From the slits in the boarded shut windows, heavy beams of light sliced the room into quadrants. In the sunny glow, thick currents of dust could were swirling to a silent orchestra. Old wooden panels creaked all on their own as the building morphed to the outside heat. The store owner licked his cracked lips and slid his hand across the counter toward his trusty shotgun.

A man was half hidden, crouched down beside a counter of canned goods and seemed deep in thought. The store owner's pa had told him to be weary of the quiet and the thoughtful. Since most thoughts were of an evil origin, it stood to reason that men most prone to thinking were of the same violent birth.

The customer had materialised there ten minutes earlier. Holstered against his hips were two long revolvers, his belt decorated with enough extra bullets to fell an entire platoon. The proprietor looked at the man's clothes. They were not something he had seen before. Leather pants and shirt, snakeskin boots, gilded collar and heels. No, whoever the customer was, he had come a long way to look at beans.

The owner's hand grasped the handle of his shotgun and tried to remember if he had loaded it since its last cleaning. His mind was fading, and his memory was hopefully the only thing to get shot that day. If he dwelled on it, he'd realise he couldn't even remember the customer opening the door and walking in.

He coughed. His throat was drier even than his crystalline lips. "Got a big trip coming up, sir?" he asked at last.

The customer did not move. "That may well be," he said with a voice too fair for his grizzled exterior. "How far from here would you say Reckoning is?"

The shop owner rolled his eyes upward to gaze at the invisible map in his mind. "Well, now, I ain't heard that name in a moment. But, hm, I'd wager you could get there in under two hours assuming your horse is fast enough."

The customer nodded. His horse was more than fast.

The owner's hand darted away from his weapon, and he placed it on the counter. Concern had usurped suspicion. "But, look now, y'don't want to go to that place, mister. It's not the town you think it is. There's a reason people quit asking about it. All sorts of oddities around that place. People missing and whatnot. Hell, even our own boy had a delivery up there and never came back. Even the sheriff won't go up there now. I'd give it a wide berth if I were you."

"Just as well I'm…" the customer began, before switching tact. "This boy who went missing. Your son?"

"Oh, nothing that serious. Just a feller what worked here for a while."

"I see. Then all is well."

The customer stood. At full height they were taller than the owner could have suspected, limbs long and wiry. It struck the owner again that it was strange he had somehow missed a veritable giant entering his place of business. The customer walked with an awkward gait to the counter, retrieved a browned sheet of paper from his pocket, and placed it down onto the counter. He dropped a pencil beside it and then pressed his index finger on the parchment.

"Thank you for your warning, but I am heading there at the behest of more concerned members of the public. If you would kindly oblige me and draw me a map to Reckoning, I would be most thankful."

"Ain't no need, mister. It's a straight line as soon as you're out the door. Just head east and keep going. I'm sure there are still some signposts to make sure you're on the right track."

The man nodded and retrieved his paper and pencil before retreating to the door. Before exiting, the owner hollered after him.

"Hey, mister, it's a long trek there. You sure you're not going to buy nothing? Been a few slow weeks around here."

The Lawman smiled. "Ah, no, no. I won't be buying anything from this store, Roger. I just wanted you to know I was in the vicinity and will be back momentarily."

"Roger? W-what you coming back here for? I've done nothing illegal."

"Oh, but that depends on whose law you abide by, doesn't it? I'll leave you to think on that." He opened the door. "Two hours each way, you say? Well, that's four hours I'm never getting back. You've got to wonder how long I'll be in Reckoning, don't you, Roger? It might do you well to sort out that mess you made before then."

"Now wait a minute, I…"

But the Lawman had gone, the door swinging shut behind him. Roger grabbed his shotgun and rushed after him. If not to shoot the man outright, then at least to proclaim his innocence, to explain his side of things. In the ten seconds it had taken him to race outside, however, the Lawman was long gone.

"Aw, horseshit," said Roger.

Scattered haphazardly along the road to Reckoning were signs with such proclamations as Reckoning: Six Mile; You Will Never Leave. These were once bright new billboards. But the paint had faded and cracked, and the wood had warped under the sun. White paint, once bright and clean, had become varying shades of green and brown as creeping vines and time itself reclaimed the boards. The road beneath the Lawman, too, had begun its slow return to nature, with thick tufts of grass breaking through the compacted soil. It must have been an enjoyable ride before…

Before? That was not something the Lawman could answer. He knew nothing of what had happened to Reckoning, only that, after three years of prosperity, it had gone mute. Become cursed. Not a soul had left the place to share its secrets.

The town was first a simple plantation. Its owner had been lucky in the land he chose for himself, and it rewarded him so handsomely he invited others to enjoy the fruits of his labour. He needed drivers and labourers, smart and capable people who could work beyond the basic field work. And with those workers came families, and with those families came fresh needs and wants, and so on, until three streets of houses sat below the plantation. And a convenience store, a watering hole, a school, and even a post office had appeared. Yes, Reckoning, by all accounts, owed a lot to the hard work of the original landowner. A lesser man would have been content with acres of private land and a few hundred slaves.

It was only when the Lawman was a mile or so outside the town his trance like musings on its history evaporated, and he remembered why he was exploring the location. From his position on the road, he could see the town, and, to a less skilled eye, all would have seemed well. The buildings showed signs of wear and needed fresh paint, but there were people tending to their properties. It was the road leading onward that concerned him at first. Debris littered the sides of the trail in increasing volume. Wagons and chests lay shattered beneath the thick bushes on either side of him.

Perhaps the people of the town had become more territorial as their land prospered. It would not be the first time and wouldn't be the last. It was often the case, the Lawman had learned, that what appeared to be a conspiracy to the outside world was often just a case of people moving on with their lives.

Still. The closer he drew to the town, the harder it was to ignore the various wreckages littering the road. Not only the carts and chests, but spent casings and torn clothing too. Charred black mounds of cinder decorated the spaces where further awning had once stood on display. More than that, though, the closer he got to Reckoning, the more the Lawman could see just how decayed the residences had become. Even the welcoming banner that hung from two iron poles had become an illegible sheet of rotten canvas.

Despite the clear signs of disrepair, the Lawman could see the hardworking folk toiling away in their lots as he entered the town. They were so busy they did not even stop to look up at him as he rode by.

He circled the small streets, hoping to get a better lay of the land should he need it. The homes, he could see, were beyond repair. Their roofs were sagging, windows broken, planks bent outward revealing rusted nails and dry rot. It was as he stared into the white and black fungus creeping up out of the floor of the post office that he reconsidered the working people. They were too repetitive. As if automatons. They carried out their menial chores with the same fluid motions with no sign of deviation. This was beyond work effort, more than being engrossed in labour.

The Lawman hopped off his horse and patted it. It whined a little and cantered away from him. He scanned his surroundings. A dozen or more people locked in their routine. In the vegetable patch outside the nearest home, he spied a woman scraping her hoe against the earth. He walked over, stooping slightly because he knew his height gave some women pause.

She was digging at nothing. Limply dragging her tool against a long-dead patch of earth. The ground was dry and faded. Two trails of scuffed ground led back to the house. She'd been working on that patch for months, it seemed.

"Ma'am?" he asked.

She did not reply. The Lawman looked at her clothes. They hung from her miniscule frame like a handkerchief caught against a metal pole. Drool was cascading out of her gaping mouth, creating a snail trail of dampness down her chin and blouse, leading to a puddle of foul liquid on the floor beneath her. Her eyes were bloodshot and crusted over, fingernails black or missing completely, hands red with oozing blisters and sores. A colony of mosquitoes were feeding on her exposed and sunburnt arms. The Lawman swatted at them, but neither they nor the woman paid him any attention.

"Ma'am? Is there someone here taking care of you? Are you in trouble? You can trust me."

She hunched forward and continued with her work. The Lawman placed a hand softly on her should as he looked over her and into her house. Her door was wide open. Inside was dark, but he could see someone in there shuffling in place. He spun and looked over at the other homes. They were no better. Men and woman in varying states of decay, skeletal and hunched, were ceaseless in their meaningless chores. The entire town was alive, if alive was truly the right word. The only place that remained calm was the plantation up on the hill. He looked up at it, saw its paint was fresh, brighter still when compared to the state of the town.

All around him, though, the people of Reckoning were wasting away. A woman was scrubbing the ragged remains of old garments in a bucket, another was tossing spoilt feed at the skeletons of chickens. Nearer to the plantation, a man limply swung an axe at a splintered pile of kindling. They were engaged in a Sisyphean punishment of some sort.

"What in the hell?" the Lawman whispered to himself. And it was hell.

He returned to his horse and grasped its reigns, walking with it along the broken roads of Reckoning toward the plantation. There was nothing he could do for the people in their yards and homes, he reasoned, until he could get to the root cause. It must have been a spell, some curse perhaps. Yes, the plantation owner had cursed the town folk, or a wandering traveller had seen fit to play one of their jokes on the place. Yes, some form of dark magick was in play, the Lawman knew that much.

He stopped. There was someone watching him, he could sense. Looking up over at the town's saloon, there was someone lingering in an upstairs window. They darted for cover as soon as the Lawman spotted them. After tying his horse to the hitching post outside the saloon, the Lawman readied his revolver and went inside.

It was dark and dank and dingy in there. It appeared almost as if the saloon resurfaced after years underwater, and the walls were slick and wet and covered in growing things. Living things and breathing fungus. Lichen. The floorboards, too, were sagging and weak, and almost gave beneath the Lawman's stride.

There were no tables in the saloon. The remaining chairs lay piled together and burnt in the centre of the room. Crystalline piles of broken liquor bottles covered the countertops and shelves. The Lawman could smell charred flesh, spoiled whiskey, fear. He walked up the stairs, being careful to keep his feet to the sides of each step.

"Hello? I saw you; you can come out." the Lawman called.

"It's not safe out there," a weary, crackled voice replied.

"I am a Merchant of Law, I can protect you."

"Tell that to them out there."

"What happened to this place?"

"I don't know."

The Lawman listened to the voice and followed it. Third door along. He pressed his hands against the wood and tried to shove it open.

"I'm barricaded in here, you fool," the voice said as if sensing the Lawman's intentions. "Leave me be. And get out of here while you still can."

"What happened to this place?"

"I told you once already, I don't know. I don't know a damned thing anymore. I can't even tell you how long I've been in this room."

The Lawman listened. It sounded like the person locked in the room was pouring themselves a drink. "Why don't you come out? We can get you some place safe in two hours. I just have to look around first."

"You won't get me out of here. There's not enough left of me to save, mister. Don't go looking to exert your merchantdom of Law or what have you in this place. There is no Law here."

"Are there others? Others who can talk? Could someone else explain what's happened here?"

"This is the last time I will tell you this: I do not know. Please leave me be. I beg you."

The Lawman stepped back and began his slow escape from the saloon. "I'm coming back for you."

"No, you ain't."

At the gates of the plantation, the Lawman found a burly man. He was larger, healthier, than those he had seen in the town itself. The man was sawing a large log, but the teeth of the saw had become blunt and rusted and so the job was as close to futile as any of the chores in Reckoning.

"Sir?" the Lawman approached him. As with the others, the man paid him no mind. But the man with the saw seemed much stronger than the others, and so the Lawman tried something. He grasped the man's scabbed wrist and tried to pry his hand away from the saw. The man's grip remained vice-like for some time, but the Lawman wrestled him free from the saw.

For a moment, the Lawman thought he had done the right thing. Freed the man from an enchanted tool of some sort. But then, after a few moments of panicked and flickering eyes followed by a brief whimper, the man collapsed to his knees and briefly swayed before falling face first into the dirt. Dead. The Lawman mumbled a few words of prayer and then looked up once again at the plantation.

Yes, it was clear something was waiting for him in that large, pillared property. The fields leading up to it were as well-maintained as the home itself. The greens were bloated and thick with regular watering, that much was clear. There were no people, though, no one was working the land of the plantation, while the town was abuzz with useless gestures and movements. It was at this moment, as he approached the plantation's colonial porch, that the Lawman realised something he had missed: there were no slaves. For a town that owed a lot to the work of such people, it was strange that not a one of them had revealed themselves. Had there been a riot? A rebellion? Had the slaves grown tired of their servitude and claimed the town they built as their own? Perhaps. Although…

If that were the case, the Lawman mused, then surely they'd be more protective of their land? Would they not have shot a giant Lawmaker on sight? And if there had been a slave rebellion, why hadn't word reached the government? If there was one thing the ruling elite disliked, it was paying their own taxes. But a close second was a slave getting lofty ideas.

The Lawman's head moved left to right to left again as he walked up the hill through the greenery. He kept expecting to glimpse a stranger lurking in the bushes, or a group of workers tending to their crops. Nothing. The rows of flora were as empty as they were well-maintained. The ground beneath his feet was damp and dark and hungry. It was too clean. No rocks or wayward tools or weeds to speak of. Immaculate land, in fact. Something even the most ardent gardener would aspire to.

He reached the black double doors of the plantation's manor and considered knocking. The white pillars on either side of him loomed high. It was a massive building, far larger than he'd expected on his approach. A rustic swinging chair creaked lightly in the breeze beside him. Potted roses and other bright flowers littered the porch. It was an inviting sight. Too inviting. The Lawman pushed open the large doors and stepped inside with his free hand hovering beside his revolver.

The decadent foyer had a tiled marble floor, black and white squares polished and iridescent. Twin sets of winding stairs led up to a balcony and a second floor. Statues and stuffed animals decorated the corners, the walls, the awnings. A bright light pooled down from the light well in the roof. The Lawman looked at the mounted heads on the walls and sneered. All herbivores. How he scorned those who refused to hunt predators. He stood in the warm glow of the light from the ceiling and surveyed his options. There were three doors on the ground floor and two above, all leading off to one side of the house or the other. But which one first? He chose the modest oaken door on the left side of the hall.

It opened up to a tight corridor, made tighter still by the rows of armour and sculptures mounted between each window. The armour appeared to belong to various peoples from various continents, with no real rhyme or reason behind their placement. Praetorian helms beside headdresses beside a samurai's red breastplate. Each door along the corridor contained a disappointment. Small rooms for coats or rifles or nothing at all.

Then came the study. Bookshelves stuffed with ancient tomes encircled the room and hid the walls. The Lawman had never seen so many books outside a library and wondered if this was how all plantations were. He ran his thumb across some dusty volumes. Latin titles and ominous feelings as he looked over them. Most seemed focused on philosophy and history, some referenced alchemy or false science, others mythology and lore. An odd assortment, as jumbled in placement as the armour in the corridor.

A desk overflowing with papers and reference guides sat in the middle of the room. Maps of the savage continents. Documents and manifests pertaining to shipments both human and not. The plantation's owner was a collector of all sorts. A scholar, too.

The next room on the Lawman's search was a museum of sorts. Several figures stood on either side of the room, looking at what must have at one time been the centrepiece. An empty, golden pedestal in the middle of the room. He could almost feel the figures watching him as he examined the area. There was nothing there except an empty sarcophagus hidden behind a broken stake of crates. If there had been a body in there, it was elsewhere.

The more he looked at the empty coffin, the more the Lawman suspected something was wrong. He looked at the floor and saw the melted remains of black candles. A chalice lay hidden between two of the wrecked crates. Magick? Perhaps. He had done well to avoid it in many of his investigations, but now and then he would come across something he couldn't explain. This was no slave rebellion or blasphemous plantation owner, that much was for certain. He stood there motionless for a moment. It felt as if the figures on the sides of the room were crying out to be touched. More magick. The Lawman laughed at himself and returned to the corridor.

The last room of that wing opened to a dark, unfinished room. It looked almost like a recent addition, built by children or primitives in the haze of a sunny afternoon. It reminded him of childhood treehouses. Three of its walls were bare and untreated wood. The fourth contained the beginnings of a mural. Again, he felt himself compelled to touch it. Before the mural was a stool and a painter's pallet. The paint was still glistening and wet.

The mural was of an arid, orange land. Strange animals roamed the land. Some hunted, others ran in groups. The trees were bent and thick, unlike any trees the Lawman had seen. Someone had drawn the outline of a family. They appeared to be indigenous tribal people. It all looked alien to him, but there was something comforting about the land, the animals, as if a beacon beckoning him home. He stood watching it for some time.

More time than he realised. For as he returned to the corridor, he could see the sun outside was low and intense. The walk to the foyer was like walking through an unfamiliar room, with the shadows of the suits of armour bowing before him. Outside, he could make out the specs of the townsfolk, still toiling away at monotonous nothing.

Lawman entered a dining room, pushing through two large doors to do so. The walls decorated with millennia of history and a country's worth of dead animals. The table stretched the length of the wide room. In its day, it must have sat a hundred or more guests. He looked closer. The table overflowed with mountains of boiled vegetables and fresh meats. The smell was overwhelming. It took the Lawman back to his days working canteens, and he could feel his stomach flip over itself. He listened. Slurping. From the far end of the table, someone was smacking their lips as they devoured everything they could. If he knew he was alone, he would have shot them immediately.

It was a bloated, older gentleman sitting at the head of the table. His family's crest decorated his massive throne. His white linen suit was bulging outward everywhere, the seams tearing open as he ate. His shirt was all but dissolved in sweat and spittle. Red pools of drool accumulated in the protracted mounds of his chest. It must have been the plantation owner. He had grown fat at an unnatural rate, if the thick, silky scars running up and down his exposed flesh were anything to go on. His face was engorged with food, and he would scarcely swallow one bite before piling in another.

The Lawman tried to ignore the piggish sounds of feasting. "Don't worry," he said, "I will get you out of here."

Unlike the people of the town, the plantation owner paused for a second, showing brief signs of cognition before gorging himself once more.

"You can hear me?" the Lawman said, not expecting a response.

One came anyway. Through the mashed grotesqueness that was the insides of the man's mouth, he hissed and sputtered something resembling his agreement, globs of gristle and sputum gushing out and down onto the table. He continued to eat, but tears were pooling in his eyes. He had a mouth but couldn't scream. Because of the food.

The Lawman approached him but halted, shocked by what he saw. The other chairs along the table were not as empty as he thought. What remained of a handsome family sat around the patriarch. They were limbless and cauterised, propped up and bound to their seats. They sat there blinking, smiling even, as the plantation owner continued to eat the meat. Not just any meat. Their flesh. They nodded as eagerly as a doting matron while the man tore into slathers of their grilled limbs.

Without thought or consideration, the Lawman levelled his revolved and shot the plantation owner in the head. The man gurgled and spewed a vile mix of blood and food onto his plate and then sank back into his chair. After taking off his hat in a moment of solemnity, the Lawman bowed at the tragic corpse. He then turned the revolved toward the closest of the guests and was about to squeeze the trigger when the plantation owner gasped, sputtered, wiped the gore from his face, and returned to his meal.

The Lawman shook his head and backed out of the dining room, closing the door shut behind him.

Most men would have left Reckoning at that point, if not several hours earlier, but the Lawman was a Merchant of Justice as he was wont to say. The living embodiment of American righteousness. And besides that, he would not receive his reward if he left without at least an explanation for the Bureau.

He knew, based on cold, hard facts and the crowded table, that whatever it was he was looking for was downstairs. In the kitchen, most likely. There was no other way the plantation owner would have access to so much cooked food. Someone was preparing the food, and from what the Lawman had seen of the people in town, they no longer had the mental facilities with which to so much as heat water. The Lawman did not dwell on his excellent detective skills.

Despite this certainty, the Lawman found his leg carrying him up the twisting stairs to the upper level. His gut had betrayed him. "Just to be sure," he caught himself whispering.

Upstairs was empty. A series of ornate bedrooms and porcelain bathtubs. It was clear, based on the portraits on the walls, that the beast in the dining room had once been a lithe, adventurous man. The photographs in the master bedroom showed a bold and determine man, more muscle than anything, poised over dead animals, exploring ruins in jungles, befriending savages of every size and colour. He was obviously a man, when he was still a man, who had built his empire from the dirt with only his own moral fortitude, an army of slaves, and major investment from European relatives. What a tragedy.

With his upstairs reprieve at an end, he could delay investigating the servant's quarters no longer. He descended back to the foyer and worked his was back to the worker's section of the house. The corridors were tight and unfinished, and the rooms overcrowded with bunk beds and cots. He realised perhaps the slaves were the first to succumb to the evil in the town. The foulest witchcraft always begins where it is least noticeable.

Finally, he found the kitchen. The stench reached him instantly. Parboiled flesh and candied yams stewing in massive pots. A roaring fire on one wall was warming a… something… attached to a metal rod. Torsos, flayed and gutted, sat in containers fun of blood-dyed salt. Blood mixed with herbs and who knew what else dripped from the chopping boards onto the floor where a mangy and desperate cat lapped it up. Cloves of garlic and onions hung from the rafters. They disintegrated to the touch as old as they were. In one pristine corner of the room, a pile of clean fine china sat waiting for future use.

In what had once been the pantry, a shrine of bones and hair covered the back wall. Red candles flitted below an old brass mask. On the floor were the unmistakable markings of a trapdoor.

The Lawman opened the trapdoor without hesitation, then stepped back. An even stronger stench invaded the room. Death. Abject death. He holstered one of his weapons and searched the room for rags, which he then tied around the gnawed femur of some unfortunate or another. Igniting it with the fire, he retrieved his weapon and climbed into the bowels of the building.

The light from the fire could only go so far, but from what he could see, the building's foundation had been dug out, reclaimed. It reminded him of a fox's den. He stepped forward with his revolver ready to fire, his nostrils burning with the stench of decay, bile ready to rise out of his throat. For the first time in a while, he noticed his heartbeat.

As he probed the darkness, it was clear that someone or something had made itself at home beneath the house. Barrels of spirits lay empty, Intricate toys and charms made from hair and teeth dangled from the floorboards above him. He could hear movement. It was almost enough for him to turn and leave. Except, as much as anything, he couldn't quite remember where the steps leading back into the plantation had gone.

A voice croaked. It came from all directions. "Have you come to kill me?"

The Lawman waved his gun around, unsure where to fire. To his surprise, his trigger finger could not move. "I don't know," he said. And he didn't.

There was a laugh from nearby. The Lawman turned and turned again. A figure stepped out into the low light of the torch. Thick, unkempt black hair, piercing yellow eyes, a face covered in ash and thumbprint runes, razorblade teeth behind an inhuman smile. The thing looked the Lawman up and down and grinned all the more. "Ah, you're not the man to kill me. Good."

The Lawman rediscovered his bravado at this and said, "Now, that's for me to decide."

The figure in the waning light shook its head. "No. No, you don't understand. You can't kill me; you're not the man I was expecting. Of course, you are more than welcome to try, but… you've seen what happens to those who try."

The Lawman holstered his weapon, which he wasn't planning on doing. He felt jovial. Convivial. Drunk. "Well, you speak very well for a, uh—"

"Creature of darkness?"

"I was going to say African."

"Ah-hah. Quite. In my time on this planet, I've learned its best to learn the tongue of any invading force. There's less chance of them thinking they have any power that way."

The Lawman stood straight and regretted it immediately. His head banged against the wood above. "So, what are you, then? You're no slave, that's for sure."

"I am the belated revenge of a continent."

"No, but really?"

The creature sighed and circled the Lawman. "I'm from an ancient race of people, I suppose you could say. I was resting in Dagbon when that pig upstairs found my tomb. He tried to coax me into being his loyal servant. But I don't respond to those requests. Least of all when I've seen what a man like that has done. Is capable of."

"He seemed like an honest man to me."

"Then you're fooling yourself. They always considered me a monster, but I never delivered suffering with such… impunity. I never enthralled the innocent or raised my hand against a child. The laws of nature apply to me just as with any creature. This man—this man—knows nothing of the natural order, or morality, of justice."

"But you are a monster, then?"

"Is that what you chose to hear? I have dealt with the real monsters of this place."

"And what of the slaves?"

"They're as free as they can be. Come, it is getting dark outside. I judge you are a man of justice?"

"It is all I am."

The creature patted the Lawman's shoulder and led him up to the plantation. "Then you know as well as I do that some of the greatest injustices have happened under the guise of legality, of destiny, of divine right. What they built this town on was injustice, and I have dealt out retribution. You have no further business here."

"But what about the people out there? In the town?"

"They were the worst of all, my friend. Not a slither of guilt between them. Even as I bent their souls to my will, they tried to convince me of their infallible innocence. So, I showed them what a life of servitude is like. No more innocents will suffer or find themselves exploited in my town. And it is my town, my friend."

"But haven't they suffered enough?"

"How much suffering is enough? How much suffering did the people they view as livestock endure? How much has my country, my land, suffered? There's a balance to be met, and we are nowhere near meeting it."

"You know, it's not just this town responsible."

"Yes, I gleaned as much. Don't worry. Soon the rest of them will be judged accordingly."

"And what of the slaves?"

"I told you, they are free. And no, they are not dead. They have become something better. Stronger. And that's more than a man of justice such as yourself can say, is it not?"

The Lawman did not answer. He didn't want to argue, and he did not want to dwell on his own inactivity. Despite his vows of Justice, he was far from a paragon of his chosen virtue. He had satisfied the Bureau's wishes, and that was all there was to it. His reports would show the town was lost, and then he would seek his next adventure. "I'll be heading out," he said to the creature.

They were standing in the house's foyer. Moonlight now oozed through the glass in the ceiling. Outside was an ever-darkening cocktail of blues. The creature held the door open for the Lawman and smiled again. In the moon's light, its visage was almost human. "Feel free to walk through town for a while. Don't tarry too long, though. I can't control what happens out there."

"I think I've seen enough, but thank you kindly."

"As you like it. If you ever stumble across someone who needs liberation, don't hesitate to direct them here. I'm a very gracious host to the right person."

"I see that."

"See you shall. Goodbye for now."

The Lawman doffed his hat and walked down the hill. He could feel the otherworldly entity watching him.

In the town, the townsfolk were putting up their tools and returning to their beds. In the morning they would wake and work again. The Lawman got on his horse and cantered by the people. For a moment, they seemed to have life in their eyes, but it was a life of shame. By the time he reached the welcoming sign, they had all disappeared back into their broken homes.

He turned to look one last time at the plantation. The figure still stood in the doorway, illuminated by the moon. In the luscious fields between the manor and the town, a sea of lightning bugs danced. They swirled in unison, circling the creature of the manor, flashing all the while.

The Lawman recognised the blinking lights for what they truly were. He gave them a bitter smile and a nod, and then he was on his way.

Of Lightning Bugs
and Sulphur

"Seems like that Lawman is a mighty chickenshit, if you ask me."
"But ain't nobody asking you, is they?"
"True enough, big man. But those lightning bugs at the end remind me of something."
"Aw hell, and I supposed you're going to tell us?"
"Of course. And unlike your story, this one really happened."

"You know, I don't think that Hastings feller knew what he was talking about."

"Well, he's an educated man and rich to boot. You'd do well to be more like him. All that happened is he understated the terrain a little."

A little. The thick, slick sludge that passed for a trail sucked at the horses' hooves and they moved onward. Trees on either side of them stood smothered and killed by hanging vines. Slick patches of dark liquid in every direction. It looked like earth after the flood had passed. Where grass should have been, only puddles and peat. The convoy's movements were a murmur compared to the incessant buzzing of mosquito swarms and the cawing carrion overhead. They may as well have been trundling through the prehistoric ages or mars, all things considered.

"Understated? This here's a swamp, Lenny. He said we'd be moving through bushland."

"I guess this is just rainy stations. I guarantee Hastings knows this land better than you. He's led no one astray. Never. What have you done?"

"Oh, not much. But here's a thing, friend, we're supposed to be heading straight west and if the sun's anything to go by, we're going all the way south."

"You're free to turn around and leave any time you want, Carl. I know it won't be the first time, and it won't hurt any of us none if you're not there when we reach our destination."

Carl bit his tongue and fell back, allowing the first three wagons to pass before he continued to move. He rode beside Marjorie and the brood. Seven children played in the back of their wagon. Only one was theirs. The other children rode with them on the pretence of it being good for the children to bond on their travels. The other six wagons got to enjoy varying degrees of peace, although to be fair, Carl did not envy the servants in their cramped confines.

He could hear the children giggling over secrets as he trotted along. There was something about the laughter of children that made all the hate in his heart dissipate. Unlike, say, Lenny, who would threaten to punch a child is they so much as guffawed near him.

Marjorie had grown accustomed to the ruckus behind her and sat dead-faced, staring off ahead of her. It took her several moments to realise Carl was looking at her. Her left hand let go of the reigns and grasped her chest as she gasped. "Don't do that! Say something next time!"

"Sorry."

"Why ain't you up front?"

"That Lenny. I know he thinks he's the boss and all, but he don't know the first thing about what he's doing. We're heading six clicks the wrong direction and if these midges don't get us, it's just a matter of time before the gators come looking."

"Uh-huh. And you told him that?"

"Yea—In so many words."

Marjorie flashed a smile of relief. "I think we should turn around while the going is still good. It'd only take us, what, two days to retrace our steps back to that old fort."

"That's assuming we can retrace anything."

Marjorie turned to the horizon. It was all the same. A flooded, deceased forest with only a little visibility in any direction. She leaned over to her side and peered at the wheels sloshing through the soup beneath. There was no trail, no proof between one moment and the next they had been moving. Their wheels would dig into the terrain and carve out little grooves, but they were just as quickly reclaimed and forgotten.

"Oh, Carl. I don't like this place one bit. This is the kind of hell mama used to talk about. Do you think you could talk to Lenny again? If not to talk some sense into him, at least to stop just long enough to move the children around. Please?"

"I can try, but I already know what he's going to say. He…" he stopped, looked at the woman he loved. "Anything for you and then some, pumpkin. I love you."

"I love you too, snakebit."

Carl rode back up toward Lenny. Despite himself, he could feel his hands slacken and his feet sag, and his horse rode slower because of it. Three other men, Fergus, Walton, and James, rode with Lenny up front, and they were talking in tones that grew hushed as Carl approached. By the time he had reached them, the three had pulled away, leaving only Lenny at the front of the convoy.

"Look, Lenny, I'm just going to level with you—"

"We're taking this route and I don't care to debate no more. You and yours are welcome to turn around whenever you so please."

"Ah, yes, but that's the problem, ain't it? We've got your children in our wagon. Couldn't we stop at least long enough to get them sorted out? Maybe someone else wants to turn back."

Lenny shook his head and sighed. "No. It's best we keep going at this time of day. We'll make it soon. I know we're all tired of this riding. Besides, where would we stop? There's not exactly anywhere to rest up around here."

As if summoned forth by the fates or something far worse, a structure broke through the mist before them. At first it appeared to be little more than a pile of boulders, but it quick became the blasphemous husk of a church. It rested on a small hill, the only incline Carl had seen in a day or more. Crab grass and gravestones surrounded it. As they drew closer, it became clear the church had been abandoned many years ago. The roof was missing shingles; the windows were shattered, the walls succumbing to the elements. The iconography on the roof was melted into crude mockeries by repeated lightning bolts over the years.

"Well, shit," said Lenny.

"I'd see this as a sign and let us stop for a while. C'mon, at least let's talk this out."

Inside, the church made the outside look pristine. The pews lay gather in a pile where the altar had been. They oozed water, eroding the ground beneath them with their continuous drips. There had been a crucifix on the wall, its desecrated remains hung redecorated with bones and jagged blades. Various animal hides had been nailed to the walls with wrought iron nails. An eternal glow of twilight broke through the shattered, boarded-shut windows, the holey ceiling, the wide-open door to the outside world. Crows called from the shadows up above. It was a temple for the forsaken and it was so itself.

The families talked for as long as they could about their choices. Most sided with Lenny, seeing no real alternative but to keep going. It was only the quiet Schmidts who wound up agreeing to turn back with Marjorie and Carl. Their young child had been the brunt of most of the prepubescent abuse during the ride and had taken this brief reprieve to hide in the graves outside. The Schmidts had also seen what mettle the others were made of during their odyssey and perhaps say the future waiting for them at the site of the new settlement. The servants, most of whom belonged to Lenny, had no say in the matter. Nor did the children, who all seemed aghast at the revelation they'd be spending the rest of the trip alone in their own wagons with their parents for company. They stood outside whining all the while, planning their eventual reunion a few days hence.

"Can we still ride together?" one of the older boys asked.

Lenny looked at Fergus, Walton, and James. They all shook their heads. "No," said Lenny. "You all climb up and try to get some rest. We should be there by sundown if we hurry." His accusatory eyes lingered over Marjorie and Carl.

Carl coughed. "Uh, just to be clear, Lenny, I make it a little after six already."

"I said sunrise. Thanks for nothing, Carl. I'd say we'll miss yous, but the truth is we'll be too busy prospering."

The four wagons were soon riding off to wherever Lenny thought their destination was, disappearing into the low mist in a matter of minutes, the echoes of their upset children the only thing breaking through the silence. The brief reprieve ended with Klaus and Louise entering, followed by the two remaining children, giggling and screaming as they ran through the faded tombstones behind the building. It was the first real, liberated laughter Carl had heard from either of them since their journey began. The Schmidts embraced each other, smiled silently at Marjorie, took some blankets from their wagon, and returned into the church.

"Calling it early, huh?" Carl called after them.

They did not answer. Instead, it was Marjorie spoke. "I guess they're staying here. We should probably do the same. I'd hate to be stuck out there in the dark."

"You mean like Lenny and them? Yeah, you're probably right? Do we have enough food to get back to where we met Hastings?"

"I'm imagining the kids got into most of it, but I've got plenty of vittles hidden away in my lockbox. We can eat big tonight and ride out on empty stomachs at dawn."

"Aw, honey, you know that's the only way to ride."

"Just wished you'd eat breakfast every once in a while, is all."

"Maybe one day. I'll meet you inside after I get our horses settled and round up Louise and the Schmidt boy. Unless… you don't think they're?"

"Hush, now, they're barely eight years old. Maybe you were a little pervert, but us sophisticated children waited until we were at least nine."

Carl watched his lady love retreat into the confines of the old church before walking around it to the back. The cemetery had more markers than he thought possible. A church in the middle of nowhere should have thirteen graves, Carl guessed. This one, however, must have had over a hundred crossed and rectangular slabs protruding from the slick, mossy ground. He could hear the children panting nearby but could not place them. They were hiding from him. Every few footsteps forward he's hear stifled tittering coming from behind one headstone. He let them play, savouring the change in pace since their rugged ride outward.

"Oh, children?" he said with singsong playfulness.

He crept along. Vaguely aware of where they were, but in no rush to find them. He looked at the graves surrounding him. Some had been dug up or otherwise unfinished. Others had sunken mounds where the coffin underneath had caved in. This was, he guessed, the norm of old cemeteries with no groundskeepers. What was not the norm, however, was what was on the gravestones. Namely: nothing. His focus on pretending to find the children gave way to confusion at the many blank markers he was surrounded by. He moved from one to the next, rubbing his hands across the stone or wood in search for faded etches, but they were each as smooth as the next. A hundred or more people lay buried beneath him in marked-but-unmarked graves. He wondered just what sort of place of worshipped they had wandered into. On top of that, he—

"Aw, you found us."

He snapped to. Crouched beneath him, pressed against one of the blank graves, Louise was looking back up at him. She seemed confused, perhaps putting an end to perceived parental playfulness. He would have stepped on her if she had said nothing.

"We have an early start in the morning, you two. We're going to need to come inside."

"Can our friend come in with us?" Klaus asked. He popped up from one of the burrowed holes he'd been hiding in.

"Friend?" Carl looked around. The other children had definitely left with their guardians.

"Oh, never mind," said Klaus. "It was a joke."

"Uh-huh. I'm sure that would go over well in the motherland, Klaus. Come on, you two, it's getting dark."

It was.

Marjorie's cooking was such that, even when made in less than stellar conditions in the middle of nowhere, its buttery aromas could overwhelm even rotten wood and airborne spores. Carl smiled as he entered the church, closing his eyes and imaging himself back home with Marjorie. The children pushed by him and found a corner for themselves, not interested in the food. Carl, however, could not resist garlic and yams.

He opened his eyes and crouched down at the small fire. "Where did the Schmidts go?"

"They're off sawing logs in the reliquary if you listen carefully. At least, I hope that's the woodwork they're doing."

Carl glanced over at the children. They were already curled up and sleeping against the wall. "Huh," he said.

"Looks like it's just the two of us, Snakebit. It's been a while." Marjorie grinned.

"That it has Pumpkin, that it has."

How they'd come to call each other Snakebit and Pumpkin was a very interesting story. They were busy getting busy in a pumpkin patch, and Carl, he—

The church doors swung open. Outside was alight with lightning. It was the other five children. They stood soaking wet and painted with the sickly greens and browns of swampland filth. Their eyes were wide and mouths agape. They stood at the threshold as if incapable of entering the building.

Marjorie was already by their side. "What's the matter, children? What happened? Is everyone OK?"

The children stood there whimpering. Only one of the older boys had the wherewithal to remember his words. "We got stopped out them and scared too, so we came rushing back here. It's safe here, ain't it, miss? That's what you were arguing without folks about. You knew this place was safe. Not like out there. No, ma'am, out there is dangerous. There's something. There's something." He lost his words and joined the others in their commiserations.

This woke up Louise and Klaus, who were happy to see their friends. They squealed and ran toward them, which was enough to make the other children forget about their worries. The seven of them were grinning and whispering to each other as they returned to their wall.

Marjorie closed the doors and gathered what few blankets she could. "You're all safe for now. Let's get you dried off and warmed up, and then we'll try to—"

"Where are your parents?" Carl interjected.

Nothing. The children were sharing private jokes and doing their best to pretend nothing had happened. Carl might as well of not existed. He stood up and pretended to help Marjorie gather some essentials. "We can't let them sleep here. I need to find the others."

"I'm not sending them out alone, Carl." She placed what she could at the feet of their guests and then walked outside to the wagon. Carl followed.

"No. No, I know. But we need to get them back. You know, I bet this is one of Lenny's ploys. They've been pawning these poor kids off on us since before we met Hastings. Tell me I'm wrong."

Marjorie tried to ignore him, fishing out the blankets and older clothes from their wagon. She stopped and looked out at the world around them. The lightning and the moon had gone, and all was black except the slither of light emanating from inside the church and the intermittent flashes of nearby fireflies. "It's pitch black out here. They'll of stopped somewhere close, just you watch. Can't be too far away if the kids got here safely."

Carl searched the wagon for tools of his own, taking his shotgun out of its hiding place. He handed it to Marjorie, who looked down at it quizzically. "If they're close, that means I can find them. Where's that lantern?"

"Up front. Why are you giving me the shotgun?"

"Just a precaution. If you'd kindly light a fire out here so I can find you."

"I don't like you going out there in the dark, honey."

"I don't enjoy being played for a rube by Lenny. Besides, you know old Snakebit's survived worse. I'll be back."

"You sure this can't wait 'til morning?"

"Either they're in trouble or their running from their responsibilities. Morning is too late either way. I love you."

"You too."

They kissed, and then Carl was on his way.

He walked like an unwanted in another man's nightmare, each footstep a guilty and tentative step into a ground that was ravenous. It was only a matter of time before his boots were slurped away. Even with the lantern attached to his hip, he could only see enough to know he did not want to see more. Each footstep came with the promise of something horrible and hostile. There was nothing for Carl to see, not of the convoy or anything else. It was more a case the air carried with it a lingering sense of dread. Only a misophonic symphony of slurps and squelches followed him.

After what could have been a decade, he came to a broken wagon wheel. It sat upright as if it had forgotten to fall. He examined the wood with his hand and could feel it was relatively new. He grabbed the lantern and scanned the area, hoping to find more of the wreckage. And he did, in time. A breadcrumb trail of splintered wood guided him toward an overturned wagon. The servants' ride. He wished he had kept the gun as he walked toward it.

The two old nags they'd been riding with lay out front, emaciated and dry beyond all reason, skin tight and sinewy, all liquid drained from inside them. Their dead, black eyes looked up at him and seemed, despite all rational thought, to be at peace. Carl circled the wagon twice, bracing himself to enter. He pulled open the flap on the rear and ducked inside, expecting to find the grizzly remains of the servants. Nothing. Instead, he found nothing. Their belongings were missing, with only the surplus luggage of the larger families left untouched inside.

Carl lingered, prying open the expensive boxes, hoping to find something he could use, but found only useless trinkets. A wagon half-full of gaudy objects that didn't even belong to the inhabitants.

When he left the wagon, he spun around, realising all too late he had lost all sense of direction. His compass proved no help as north was purportedly every direction he turned. There was no trail to retrace his footsteps. Carl knew his only option was to run like a madman toward any light he could see. He ignored his instincts and continued to move what he could only assume was forward.

Creepy onward, Carl expected to see more debris. Proof, perhaps, one of the other wagons had been waylaid. It startled him when he looked up and saw a tall figure standing not too far ahead of him. He aimed the lantern at it, his free hand clenched into a fist. The figure did not move. As he approached it, he could see just how tall it was. It loomed over him with giant, spindly arms. A tree. He had almost forgotten trees existed. Looking up at its gnarled, leafless branches, he tried not to gaze beyond it into the heavens as heaven was not something he wanted to think about alone in the dark.

Getting closer still, his heart leapt into a frantic beat. The tree was moving close to the base. Or something was. Writhing in the blackness. He inched forward, finding another emptied horse by his feet. It had put up more of a fight than the servants' horses, as the surrounding filth was scraped and spattered. Then something moaned.

Carl returned his gaze to the tree and was met by shimmering eyeballs. James' body was splayed and displayed on the tree, his arms nailed to two of the lower branches. His shirt was torn apart, his stomach disembowelled, intestines inching downward to the dank earth below.

Carl approached him. He had cared little for James in life and so found it hard to mourn his death. The man had been left as a trophy, however, and Carl knew enough to know people left as ornaments for no reason. No, you leave a trophy out for the living to find. To appreciate. To fear. He had to get back to the church. To hell with the others.

"Sorry it came to this," Carl mumbled.

James gargled and convulsed just as Carl was about to turn around. Snakes poured out of the poor man's stomach, hissing as they dropped to the ground and slithered away. James, who had appeared dead, snapped forward and stared at Carl. "Help," he whispered.

It was dark out. Marjorie had been lying to herself about the time. Convincing herself it was still twilight. That she'd only kissed Carl's lips but five minutes ago. That he would be back in a moment. Her façade was fading fast.

The children had giggled and mumbled to each other for some time, like old friends meeting for the first time in years, before falling asleep. In their hiding place, the Schmidts continued to snore, oblivious to the world around them. Marjorie was all alone with her lies.

The fire!

She couldn't deny the passage of time any longer and felt the trembles of inwardly directed fury as she stomped outside. Her denial had doomed her dear husband.

Stepping outside, she saw the fog was gone, and the sky had transformed into a bountiful harvest of heavenly bodies. A thousand thousand sparkling gemstones illuminated the world around her. The orange moon, full and resplendent, hung low on the horizon. The ground surrounding the church's hill was a reflective obsidian mirror, a never-ending surface mimicking the spectral sky above. Waves of light wafted over the terrain, insects calling out to each other in their own ephemeral way. Marjorie could see off into the great forever, but the surrounding land contained nothing but the idle figures of dead trees, standing upright and terrified like frightened hostages. No Carl. No anything.

She found herself short of breath and mesmerised and quickly broke free from the view to turn her attention to the fire. A pile of wood and kindling sat there, and all she needed to do was light it, but the fire wouldn't keep. Small puffs of foul grey smoke would fly off temporarily, but she couldn't make the fire stay for five or six attempts until finally some glowing proximity of a proper fire remained. It was barely enough to heat her morning coffee, much less bring her man home, but it was a start.

Marjorie hummed and hawed, looking first at the church, which seemed to have regained its former glory in the glow of night. It offered nothing to help her. The wood inside was spoilt and useless, and anything she could consider kindling was too important to part with. She turned her attention to the tapestry of starlight above and below her. Maybe there was something nearby that could help? Yes. She could retrace her steps easily, and a few reeds would be enough to help the fire take.

She stepped back into the gutted church and crouched beside the sleeping Louise, stroking her cherubic face. Her daughter would be fine for just a minute. The three of them had such bold plans for their new life that they'd almost forgotten the life they'd already created. Marjorie smiled.

When she returned to the outer darkness, the landscape had morphed somehow. While the stars still shone bright, and the wet ground echoed their sentiments, a gravel path had appeared at the bottom of the knoll. It was illuminated on either side by rows of burning beacons and trailed off to a glowing something not too far away. Whatever it was, was beckoning her toward it, and she knew better than to defy dark magick. She walked without hesitation onto the path and made her way to the bright light. The church behind him vanished in an instant. The ground crunched underfoot. She'd forgotten how that felt, the land around her as cannibalistic and wet as it was.

As she walked, she looked over the flames out into the darkness where the trees had been. There in the blackness appeared the fading images of faces, some known to her, others not. The convoy she had written with, for instance, was that them? Look at her through the shroud of darkness. Their features looked the same, at least. Marjorie called out to them but they remained motionless, half lost to the abyss, off-white, unblinking eyes the only part of them that even felt real. There were whispers, to be sure, but they did not seem to be directed at her, or even belonging to the moment she was trapped in, but the lost echoes of forgotten memories.

She continued onward, trying to null her senses by focusing on the path ahead.

The light at the end of the trail fizzled as she drew closer. No longer some blinding ball of energy, it took on a new, tangible home. A house. A log cabin. It was the sort her elders from the old country had warned her to avoid. Would that she had a choice. Smoke gushed out of the building's chimney, its windows glowing with candlelight, the door leading inside open wide. No. Not a door, but a mouth agape, with the remnants of old meals still hanging from its arched top. And the windows, she could see, were more like eyeballs gazing down at her.

Nevertheless. On she went.

Inside the house was nothing like the outer cabin, rather a series of long, empty marble corridors that took Marjorie down toward a massive dining room. It belongs to a lost, mythological era, as best she could see. There were no rooms like that in her America, at least. Statues on either side of the room seemed to tell a story of their own.

In the centre of the room was a long table. Empty. At the far end, a wizened, miniature woman was sitting on a large table. She was looking up at a tall figure in a dark suit, but Marjorie couldn't see him properly. His hand rested on the woman's shoulder for a moment and then he vanished, leaving only the crone and Marjorie. The woman weakly looked up at Marjorie. Her eyes were cavernous and a midnight blue, her skin little more than a series of scars and wrinkles. She smiled a toothless smile but said nothing.

"Uh, ma'am," said Marjorie, her manners always the last thing to leave her, "I was wondering if you could help me and mine? We're not from these parts and my husband is lost out in the swamp. I was hoping you might know how to help him so we can go home."

The woman blinked and nodded. "But you are home."

Carl ran. He ran to where, in accordance to all logic, the broken carriage should have been. It was not there. Nothing was. He continued to run even as his stomach could feel the digging pressure of a thousand invisible and scorching daggers, even as his outward breath was shallow and desperate and airless, even as his boots were claimed by the hungry and malevolent ground beneath him. He stumbled forward and crawled through the thick soup, all too soon wading his was across the ground with desperate, erratic flailing movements. There was nothing to be seen around him. The mist had grown heavy and omnipresent, walling him off from the rest of the world in a sinking prison cell all his own.

He was sinking. Sinking into the peat swamp. His vision stung as brine and who knows what else splashed against his gnarled face. Dark and dreadful shapes unfurled in the grey fog. Hissing. He could hear hissing. Chanting. Marjorie, his thoughts turned to Marjorie, her smile, her laugh, her beguiling charm. This was it, he thought, and if he was damned to never see his love again, the least he could do was worship her image.

Something grabbed the collar of his shirt and hoisted him onto firm land.

Lenny stood over Carl as he spat out sludge and thanks in equal measure. His rescuer's clothes hung from his thin limbs in rags, his eyes haunted. In a few hours, Lenny had grown a thick beard. Carl stared at him, barely recognising the root cause of his problems. Behind them stood two others, familiar but changed. Fergus and Jenny, Walton's wife. The three of them looked down at Carl with a mixture of shock and concern. They were grasping heavy branches like clubs, poised and ready to strike should they need to.

Carl showed them his mud-spattered palms as if to appease them. "Thank you. Thank you. You saved me."

"That remains to be seen," said Lenny. "But we thought you'd be long gone from this place by now."

"I couldn't leave just yet. Your children found their way to the church before we could head out. Didn't seem right leaving them there."

"The children!?!" Jenny let out a laugh. It was her first laugh in ages, rattling in her throat like loose change in a can.

Lenny lifted Carl to his feet and wrapped his arms around him. "Oh, thank you! Thank you, Carl! After all these months, we'd assumed they'd... but they're alive? Oh, praise be!"

"What do you mean months? We parted ways this evening."

Lenny shook his head. "Maybe for you. But this place. It's not real. At least not as far as faith or science tells us. We've been out here for months. You were right, Carl. You were right all along. That Hasting's lad sold us a crock of shit and we ate it up like hungry dogs."

Carl inspected the three of them. They had aged terribly. Their clothes were loose. "What happened out here?"

Lenny did not or could not answer. Carl looked over at Fergus and Jenny, who were just as unobliging with their answers. If they had the words to explain what they had experienced in the swamps, they were lost in the purgatory of their psyches.

"I, uh, I found James," Carl said.

The three did not answer with words, but their shudders were all he needed.

"He was still alive. Who... what did that to him?"

Lenny raised one finger in the air and spun it around. "This place is something else."

"I've noticed."

"But have you? It's alive. Can't you feel it feeding off you? We are in the beast's belly and it has swallowed our souls. We're all that's left."

Jenny stepped forward. "But our young'uns are at the church, you said? That means there's still hope."

Fergus agreed. "We thought we lost them weeks ago. Can you take us to them?"

"I hope so," said Carl. And he did. Hope so, that is.

The old woman of the breathing house ushered Marjorie to sit beside her. The hall had turned small, cosy. A fireplace roared nearby. The table was small and round and covered in sweets. Marjorie took a handful for the children, palming them into one of her many pockets. The old woman observed this, and her face contorted into something resembling approval.

"What did you mean when you said I'm home?" Marjorie asked at last.

"Just that. This is your home now." The old woman's voice was tinged not only with an ancient melancholy but a hint of the old country. She talked like Marjorie's mother talked and how she'd insisted Marjorie didn't. Something about the flatness to the syllables. Marjorie found a strange comfort with the familiarity. It change and nothing, though.

"If this is home, where's my husband? My daughter?"

"Yes, yes, very good," said the hag.

Marjorie could feel the building move. Rock, even, as if it were doddering along doing its chores.

"The servant's. Now, I don't know if they even got gotted, because we never saw them disappear, they just did one day. So we thought the same thing must have happened to our children."

"And then?"

"Well, then we got picked off one by one, obviously. It came in our sleep or plucked us up off the ground without warning. Never more than one at a time. And here's what's strangest of all…" Lenny fumbled over his words.

They were walking in single file toward nothing. Carl had to maintain the pretence of knowing where he was going. His old friends had lost it. "Strangest of all?"

"Oh! Well, you for sure noticed this beard of mine. It feels like we've been out here since last year some nights. But nights isn't the right word for it. No, there're no nights here. No days, neither. Just time trapped in place. Like us."

"How long we been walking, anyway?" Fergus called out. They turned to face him. He looked tired of the three of them. Three?

"Say, wasn't Jenny right behind you?" Lenny asked.

The house swayed violently, as best Marjorie could tell. Nothing else in that dining room seemed to notice. The old lady, the table, the fire, all stayed in place, immovable and indifferent to the earthquake. Marjorie swayed with the movement, struggling to grab onto something, only to see a flash of light and feel a hand against her writer. It was the old lady's hand, wart-blossomed and cankered, not there for reproach but for comfort. All at once Marjorie felt at ease in the moving home. She imagined she was in a boat in a storm; which was closer to the truth than she could ever know.

It must have happened when her eyes were closed, but Marjorie was sitting at the table facing the old woman. Up close, there was an ambiguous glare to the woman's eyes, as if she was capable of many contradictory things. She looked saintly and malevolent. Her long, grey nose hung over her mouth, which was just as hidden by the folds and creases of her sagging skin, but to Marjorie's mind she was trying to look reassuring.

"We go get children now! And then husband! Oh, but one important thing: is he a good man?"

"I wouldn't of married him if he weren't."

"Yes, yes, lots of people say that. But truly?"

Marjorie cast her mind back to the many deeds of Snakebit. The caresses, the kindness, the love. "He's as good a man as can be, given the circum-stances."

"So not worth the rescuing?"

"He is to me. You can't just throw around words like 'good' or 'bad' and expect them to stick, ma'am. Nothing is wholly one or the other. Even my old daddy used to care for injured bunnies."

The old woman looked at her.

"And besides which, are you good yourself? Seems to me like someone in a moving house shouldn't be throwing stones."

"Ah, but I am the one in the moving house. But just as you say, your words are true. We shall see the man your husband is."

The three men ran ever onward to a faint glow in the distance. It was the only beacon they had, and given the alternative of standing still, running seemed like the way to go. At least for a minute.

Fergus sprinted ahead of the others and had been since Jenny's disappearance, only to stop, abruptly lurching forward with both hands clasping at his gut. Lenny pushed him to one side as he continued his run, sending the distraught man to the ground. He lay there rolling in the slush with his fingers digging deeply into his own flesh. His cries were not English. They were barely human. Carl crouched beside him.

"Run you fool!" Lenny called out, already vanished into the mist.

Carl lowers his hands to Fergus' side and tried in his own way to help, but the man was convulsing and thrashing about so violently that Carl had no choice but to step be. He stood there, trying to think of a way to help, until Fergus removed his hands from his gut.

Something was drilling its way into his chest and hands. Red leeches with corkscrew suckers winding their way inward. They were everywhere. Carl stepped back once again as Fergus held his dissolving hands out for help. Carl ran.

He ran screaming for Marjorie until he heard his name calling back to him. Not Marjorie's voice. Not a woman's voice. Lenny. Carl followed the sound of the voice and found the man half submerged in a pool of black tar. It was pulling him down, and he grasped the dead reeds of a nearby tree.

"Carl! Pull me out!"

Carl looked at the fallen idiot and then up over at a glowing green light. A fire. Marjorie's fire. He almost ran toward it.

"Carl, you can't just leave me here."

Carl nodded. He stepped tentatively to where the black sludge seemed to end and stood in place. He could feel Lenny's fingers try to climb up his bare feet to his ankles, the hems of his pants, trying in vain to pull himself out of the bottomless pit of sludge.

"Carl?" Lenny stared at the motionless friend.

"This is all your fault," Carl said. He pulled his foot free from Lenny's probing flirtations and raised it high, stomping once, twice, three times on the man's head. Lenny spat and sputtered and swore, and Carl could feel his gnashing teeth try to sink themselves into the sole of his foot. But the only thing sinking was Lenny. Carl continued to stomp until the sludge almost claimed him.

Lenny's hands were all that remained. They twitched and shook as they worked their way down into the abyss.

Carl stood there but for a moment. The green light was calling to him. Marjorie was waiting. He could feel lit. He would see her once again.

Some say you can still hear him calling out in those forsaken Badlands.

For a Favour

"Now just wait a moment. Who told you that story was true? Doesn't sound to me like there were any witnesses left standing."
"Oh, hell, it could have been one of the kids."
"Yes, I'm sure one of them figured it all out. A walking house? A swamp that's really a stomach? And a child escaped with the complete story?"
"Do you have a story or are you just going to flap your gums all day?"

Widow Slocombe was having the hardest time lugging the supply crates to her cart. The store owner did not want to help her because of his hobbled leg, the servant boy had taken sick, and her brother, the honourable pastor, was preparing for yet another funeral. Sad times had come to stay in the town of Marston.

She only needed to move the boxes a short distance, but they were too heavy. She looked around for potential witnesses of her imminent embarrassment, and stoop over low enough to drag the first crate along the uneven planks. It made it over the first few slats and the widow could feel herself smiling as she huffed and pulled. The next plank, though, jutted upward and caught the crate and before the good widow Slocombe knew what had happened she was pulling at thin air and toppling backward onto the ground exposing her shame for any potential onlooker.

From her position on the ground she could see the blustery, warm sky overhead was being eaten by thick rain clouds. Just great. She'd need a miracle to get back to the house before the heavens opened. And even if she made it home, it was clear she was about to spend a week in doors with only her brother for company as the sins of the last season were washed away.

It happened every year.

She stood up and cursed at the crate and was about to do the same for the broken Old Jerry watching her from the window of his store, when she noticed a young man leaning into the nearby shadows. She smiled at him, tried to get his attention, but he made a brief game of pretending not to notice. Her widowdom did strange things to people. She was a young, attractive woman with a few good years ahead of her, but her name was marred with a multitude of deaths. And what a shame it was, some older women in town would say, but for the dead husband and parents and such young Annie Slocombe could have had her way with any number of rich, continental suitors.

But the man in the shadows wasn't from Marston, and she hoped her charms were not so out of practice that she couldn't coax him into hauling a few heavy boxes.

"Say, mister, could you…" she began.

He hadn't been pretending to ignore her at all. Her words sent his head spinning, and he turned to face her with the clunky awkwardness of a too-smart city boy, more familiar with his wet nurse and Athena than a woman his own age.

"Huh-hmm? Y-yes ma'am?"

His voice was refined, like fancy wine. He was not from Marston. Annie Slocombe pointed at her crates and found her voice lilt upwards as it did whenever she met a new man.

"Could you help me lift these up? It seems my strength has abandoned me for the day."

"I'd be much obliged to help you, ma'am, but then you would owe me."

She laughed and looked him once over. His suit was new, his boots alligator of all things. More importantly, he had the face of a kind man, the sort usually reserved for old saints and hermits. "I sure would owe you mightily. I need these things at home before the rain sets in."

The man picked up the first crate and smiled. It seemed weightless in his arms. "So we are in agreement, you owe me a boon."

He dropped the crate into the cart and then turned to stare into the widow's eyes. He waved off his comment and let out a happy puff of air as the left corner of his mouth crept upward.

Annie paused, not wanting to reiterate once again that she owed him. It was often the way with young people that they repeat the same unfunny joke until the point of nausea, and Annie refused to do that. Again. The man stood there staring at her and she felt naked before him. It was the first time she'd stared into a man's eyes since.

Since.

"Oh, but bless you for helping me. Lord knows I needed a miracle today, and here you are mister—" she trailed off. Something had grabbed her hand. She looked down. The man was shaking her fingers.

"Mister Cross, ma'am, a pleasure," he said. "It's always a delight when my end of the bargain is so light, Annie. Is there anything else I can do for you?"

He released her hand and lifted the remaining boxes.

She could feel her chest expand erratically as she tried to catch her breath. Was she blushing? Her cheeks felt warm. Her eyes, too, as she was watching the stranger carrying her supplies like they were balloons.

"I said, is there anything else I can do for you?"

She was definitely blushing. "Oh! Oh! No, no thank you. That's all right. But perhaps if you're in town, I will see you again. That's provided you'll be here for a while."

He winked. "I'll be here a lifetime."

She tilted her head forward, hoping to hide the grin and the glow beneath the shadow of her hair. This was to be the seven hundredth time she had climbed onto the cart, but with Mister Cross' eyes still on her, she almost forgot herself. She climbed weakly into the seat, moving like a fainting drunk, and paused. The only thing matching the knots in her stomach was the paranoia someone was watching her. Watching them. She didn't want to leave Mister Cross alone just yet, but knew what lingering would do to his unsullied reputation. Men who talked to the Widow Slocombe for too long in that town didn't stay there for long.

"I'll be seeing you," he called out as she rode off.

Annie smiled as she took that old ass home.

The first blast of thunder came within seconds of her emptying the last crate into the pantry. She ran outside as the first drops of rain came down, and unhitched her donkey, slapping it softly in the hopes it would trot off to the barn. It refused, standing there braying instead, even as the few exploratory droplets gave way to a downpour. Annie escaped back indoors before she was too wet.

Outside, the growing storm rumbled. All it did was remind her just how empty the building was. It was akin to being trapped in a bottle in the ocean, she thought. Her thoughts didn't linger on overly poetic metaphors and similes for long. No. Once she was certain she was alone in the house, the young widow Annie Slocombe turned her thoughts to Mister Cross. She pressed her fingers against her wet lips, imagining them to be Mister Cross' mouth. Fantasising about future meetings, of a romance yet to come, Annie thought back fondly to the hankerings of early attractions, back when such things were possible for her. Death does more than take the living from you, she mused, it also robs you of once cherished memories, activities, feelings. Inclinations. Her husband's brutal death had buried the prospect of loving again right beside his shattered remains. Marston's other residents killed any lingering hope, them and their beady, judgmental eyes.

She sat alone with her hands and her thoughts of Mister Cross and was about to delve into deeper daydreams before her brother burst through the front door, covering his head with a bundle of papers.

"That ass needs to be tied up or it will escape," he mumbled before retreating to his private study. The door locked behind him.

Annie's brother was a man of few words when there wasn't a bible in front of him. Annie often wondered if he even had words of his own left in that bulbous head of his.

Her libidinous mood had vacated, replaced by a disappointment and resentment that lay dormant in her at even the best of times. It was true that her life was easier than many widows, and many people, but in some ways, it felt as if she were already dead. At least in suffering, you know you are alive. Annie did not even have that luxury—far be it for her to suggest suffering was a luxury—and instead had to life of solitude. She was her sexless, joyless brother's caregiver, a prisoner in his keeping, in a town that reviled her because she was neither a virgin nor a married woman. Not that either was her fault.

Ah, but Mister Cross, she caught herself thinking, as if to placate her boiling frustration. There was a man with big city ways and the means to get her out of her purgatory. She could leave with him on the pretext of marriage, perhaps, and then disappear into the din of the civilised world. Nobody would be any wiser. And as for Mister Cross, those sophisticated city men understood that rescuing a woman didn't mean that you got her as your prize.

How she hoped to see him again. They already had private jokes about favours, which on its own was enough for Annie. She had made as much an impression on him. Her lips broke into a smile and she allowed herself to collapse back into the rocking chair until the clattering from her brother's study compelled her to finish her errands.

She scrubbed down the common areas and prepared the vegetables and other essentials for the week ahead. She swept and dusted and polished. The fun stuff. Outside, the storm went from strength to strength, sounding like a war-zone from a future decade. Blue electric light flashed through the cracks in the shutters and from under the doors. Annie had forgotten about the donkey entirely, and of Mister Cross.

Her brother hadn't left the study once to check on her, or to offer help. Far be it for him to live by his pontificated virtues. The virtuous and veritable widow Annie Slocombe wondered if perhaps he was searching for a passage that would allow him to cast her off. While she was the only one to maintain the house after the last caretaker perished, she was also as close to an albatross around his neck as she was his. He was the town's preachers, and Annie was Annie, and all that entailed.

There was a knock at the door. Annie ignored it, assuming it was the wind bashing the boards outside. But then it came again. Louder. More distinct. Three deliberate knocks.

Annie did not reach the door in a hurry, but the instant she unlatched it and opened it, she wished she had reached it sooner. The wind was fierce, and the torrent of rain threatened flash floods, but standing just outside the door was Mister Cross. He did not seem the least bit fazed by the weather, standing motionless and erect, his glowing eyes staring straight into Annie's, as if he knew in advance where she would stand. Widow Slocombe found herself unable to speak, stuck in time in a protracted, baited silence.

At what felt like five minutes and a thousand flutters of her convulsing heart, she found herself. "Where are my manners! Come in here at once, Mister Cross!"

He removed his hat and entered the abode. Annie rushed to find him a warm blanket, but when she returned his clothes were dry. Unblemished, even. Mister Cross drifted around the entrance of the house with his thumbs kneading the brim of his fedora.

"Please, please," Annie said, pointing to the fire with an open hand as she walked toward it.

Mister Cross obliged. He stood by the hearth and gazed into the fire. His hand plucked the nearby poker from its resting place and began the stab at the embers.

"I can take your gloves and coat, if you like," Annie began, then bravely ventured "That is, if you intend to stay for a while."

He turned to face her. It seemed as if the fire's glow lingered in his dilated pupils. "That's won't be necessary, my dear. I have no idea how long I will be here tonight."

Tonight? There was a whisper of a promise in the way he said that. "But the rain, Mister Cross! You can't go back out in that, surely. Is there anything I can get you? A drink? My brother?"

"I came here to see you, actually, Annie."

"Oh, Mister Cross! Never in my wildest—" She stopped herself. Her hand wasn't the only thing she was exposing. She inhaled, tried to personify the word demure as she returned to the rocking chair. Mister Cross stood in place and then sat in her brother's seat beside the fire. He sat there with the effortless confidence of someone who had always sat there. Gone was his flubbed speech and stiff nature. "Is anything the matter, sir?"

"That depends on you, doesn't it?"

Something unfurled deep inside her even as she bit on the insides of her cheeks. "How do you mean?"

Mister Cross' inviting lips morphed into an enticing smile. "Your promise at the general goods store in town, Annie. I am here to call in my boon."

Annie looked over at her brother's study guiltily before laughing. "Of course. Anything you want."

"Anything, Annie? That will be the second time you've made this promise."

"Of course, Mister Cross. I am here for you in whatever manner you do so desire." She puckered her lips, not out of some sad attempt to appear seductive, but because she reconsidered the words, she had used about ten seconds too late. She looked down at the fire."

"Good," said Mister Cross. He stepped up out of his chair and approached the good widow. Her heart was racing more than even she thought possible. She tilted herself forward to meet him and was surprised and then confused in short order when he sunk his hand deep into his pocket and retrieved a bowie knife. "I need you to take this here knife into your brother's study over there," he pointed like a field general giving orders, "I need you to go in there with this knife and slit your brother's stinking throat."

She took the knife as the joke she assumed it to be and dropped it by her feet, grasping Mister Cross by his fingers, hoping to tug him forward. He did not move. "You... you aren't serious!" She laughed. Such a buffoonish joke. She sure knew how to pick them. Her old husband had been the local jester before he exploded.

Mister Cross shook his head. Annie let go of his hand and her hopes of entwinement.

"You can't expect me to kill my brother. Not least of all because I don't even know you, mister."

"But you see, I can assure you I do expect you to kill your own brother. That's three times now you've promised to do anything I ask. I can assure you this world and the next do not look favourably one people who renege on their vows."

Annie stood up and shoved Mister Cross to one side, walking back to the front door. "You moved two boxes! That hardly equates to murdering my sole remaining kin."

Mister Cross stooped to pick up his knife. "Irrelevant. I asked if there was more you wanted, and you refused my further help. But I am not so selfless, Annie. Not by a long shot."

Annie unlocked her door once more. Opening it a crack, she could hear the storm outside was unrelenting. She pushed it closed again and turned to face her guest, looking at him, the study, the fire, the blade, one after the other until she felt dizzy. "If you want him dead so bad, why don't you go do it yourself? I won't stand in your way. I won't even tell the sheriff your name."

Mister Cross' face turned as grim as the Reaper's. "No, that won't do. It won't do at all. I will abstain from boring you with the details, my dear Annie, but I am forbidden from killing a man of the cloth."

"Ha. You're too scared to kill a preacher your own self so you're making a poor old widow woman do it for you? You're not barely a man. And, what, you think because you lifted some boxes for me I'm obligated to do your dirty work?"

Mister Cross stepped closer, all but touching her. His eyes were pools of onyx, his gums were bloodied from clenched teeth, his nostrils flared like a cornered animal. "You and I are united by oaths, my dear. Just as you were with your husband. Without our word, the world would descend into chaos. Our word is the only good thing left on this plane of existence. I made a vow never to kill a man of the cloth, and you promised you would do anything I asked. Three times."

"No. I refuse. This is a sick game you're playing. Kill him yourself or get the hell out of my home one, but I won't be sucked into your sad puppet show, mister."

His right hand shot up and grasped her tenderly by the side of her face. In a flash, she could see another world. No. She was in another world. An icy frost tore into her exposed flesh as she stood on the edge of an icy mountain. All around her, half-frozen lepers wailed as they tried to claw their way out of the frozen ground. Beneath her, a sheer drop into a volcanic maw. Giant lumbering figures moved down there, stoking the flames and supporting the rock-face. She looked up and could see no sunlight or heavens, only a never-ending ascent through a treacherous and ragged mountain. The din of moaning and screaming was deafening, and if she remained there for but one moment more, she knew she would go made. Just one more second of pure suffering.

She sat at the table in the kitchen. It had come with the house. Built by a blind carpenter, or so the story went. Mister Cross sat facing her, his hands admiring the contours of the well-built table.

"Ah, you're back," he said.

"What sorcery was that?"

"If you do as I ask, you will never have to find out. And as we have established, my word is bond, Miss Slocombe."

"But why? Why kill him?"

"For me? No reason. It's just something I want done. But you? Let me count the ways, Annie. Your brother is nothing but a thorn in your side. You're a lion, Annie, and I want to set you free. Haven't you thought about it? Weren't you thinking about a future in the big city just today?"

"Yes, but—"

"But nothing. Annie, your life has been on hold since that unfortunate accident with, what did you call him, oh yes. Ever since Nathaniel and your brood were lost to you—"

"How did you know his—"

"He left a hole in your heart, love. And your brother in there, the turbulent priest, has robbed you of a chance to find it. This town hates you, Annie. Your own brother hates you. But in the big city? That may be another story altogether. Forget what I am due, don't you owe it to yourself to break free?"

He pushed the knife once more toward her. She grasped it and stood up. Something gave her pause. Mister Cross was not a good person. She lingered over him. He looked up at her and smiled.

"Try it."

She did. The blade sank into his neck with ease and he grasped and the severed artery with futile, flailing motions as he collapsed onto the floor. Annie stepped backward and watched him convulse and sputter out. She didn't know what to do. Her brother might. She turned to approach his study and then heard laughter behind her.

Mister Cross returned to his feet, the blade still protruding from his throat. He was smiling his damned smile. Annie could not move if she wanted to. And she did. The thing calling itself Mister Cross removed the blade from its body. Not a drop of blood had been spilt.

Annie fell to her knees, her limbs limp and useless. She looked up as the man made his way toward her. His smile was permanent, his eyes two fiery balls of cinder. He dropped the blade one last time at the angelic widow Slocombe.

"Annie, that was good. Now you know you can do it. And more besides. Now, you have a few options. All but one road leads to that frozen mountain, so I would warn you not to be too rash here. You could easily open yourself up right now and put an end to our little game, but you know where you would find yourself. Similarly, you could just do nothing. But, again, we know how that ends. There's only one way to save yourself this night, Annie, and we both know deep down in that heart of yours it's what you really want. Rest assured your brother will die tonight, by one means or another. But only you can save yourself. I knew the moment I met you, you were something else, Annie, so please don't make a fool out of me. This is my gift to you."

With that, he retrieved his hat from beside the fireplace and stepped out into the howling rain. The door closed behind him.

The Widow Slocombe sat there looking at her reflection on the blade. She looked so fragile staring back at herself. In her mirrored image there was nothing of the woman she told herself she was. Her fingers wrapped themselves against the hilt of her weapon. She stood. Part of her expected Mister Cross to return as one ultimate joke. She paused there, waiting for him to reappear. Nothing came. The room was empty once again. The fire and the storm outside were both dying.

And only her brother's snores echoed through the walls.

A Forest Whispers

"So? Did she do it? Did she kill her brother?"
"Now how in the hell am I supposed to know?"
"I just thought—"
"That's enough of this, fellas. This here's a true story. There's even an ending."

Angus was beginning to think he should have stayed with the other boys his age. But no, he had to give a bombastic speech to his old man about how he, too, was a man. A small man who couldn't grow a beard and whose balls hadn't dropped, but a man nonetheless. He wasn't, if he was honest. Deep down, he knew he was still a boy who wet the bed and pretended the wood chips next to the lumber pile were toy soldiers. Yet, despite his prepubescent limitations, he'd insisted, to the point of asphyxiation, that he would accompany the menfolk to their new patch of land.

This outburst alone was enough to convince his pop he was ready to work hard and put hair on his chest. And what a complete mistake that had been. There he was, in the wilderness, on a muddy patch of land surrounded by lumber and inhabited exclusively by people twice his age who hated him. A few tents, some tools, and nobody to play with were all young Angus had for proper company.

It wouldn't have been so bad, maybe, if his brother wasn't already the tallest person in the camp, wasn't already hauling in long rods of timber with his thick arms and thicker beard. Everything his brother did was a display of strength, and since not a man in their camp could beat him, they directed their attention to the closest facsimile. Namely, one Angus.

Angus couldn't lift trees, was useless with a hammer, and had given up trying to defend himself. Sometimes he could stand on a ladder and follow basic instructions, but even that was a 50/50 bet, because every so often his ears would go wobbly and then so would he. The older men yelled at him before, during, and after any attempt to complete a task. Because he should have stayed with the other boys.

And none of the men were the playful sort who would play with him after the work was done. They were all dour and angry and drunk, and if they weren't busy building the town, they were busy cussing up a storm and arguing about which of their wives was the most something or other Angus couldn't quite understand.

By the end of the first week, the men had settled the foundation of three buildings and cut half of the wood they needed down to spec. The adults demoted Angus to dog wrangler after two days, which wouldn't have been the worst job in the world except they only had one dog and it was deaf. What this meant for Angus was he would mostly just sit on a grassy knoll outside the infant town's perimeter where he would whittle and whistle and otherwise wile the while away.

The truth he kept himself from saying was he missed home. He missed his mother and sisters most of all, but he also missed playing with the other boys and chasing the girls around asking to see their legs and things. The boys would group together in parks and show off muscles they didn't have and coax each other into entering dark and haunted places. Then they'd go home to their warm homes and warmer beds. Yes, he missed them too, having only a canvas triangle and a campfire to call home.

On one of the many days Angus was out in the thick grass, he was busy listening for snakes and ticks. Quite how he expected to hear a tick was anybody's guess. He liked to crouch in a patch of reeds he'd found and watch the bigger men work, pretending he was a scout for a local tribe or a desperado seeking refuge. There was a bonus to this game. If they couldn't find him, they couldn't yell at him and try to get him to do grunt work. And if he couldn't do grunt work, he couldn't mess up, and then they wouldn't yell at him again. It was the perfect game.

He was in the reeds wearing a crown of twigs the first time he heard it.

"Hello," a tiny voice called out to him.

In response, Angus did what anyone would do and promptly ran away. He spent the rest of the day hiding motionless in his tent hoping nobody would come looking for him, and it was a useless nope, because nobody cared enough to come looking for him. He should have used his hope for something less redundant, like going home, or for waking up twice as tall as anyone else around.

The next day, Angus avoided the reeds entirely. Not because he feared the tiny voice, though. He'd just spent too much time playing in the same spot, was all. It got boring, and he needed a fresh adventure.

So, he played around the dead tree on the other side of the encampment where people could rush to him if they needed him for anything. The ground around the tree was tough and just as lifeless as the tree itself. He had to be careful playing there because if he fell there would be no grass to save him. Climbing the tree was out of the question, too, because the branches would probably break and then he'd be right back down on the ground dealing with that situation. A shame, too. Angus tried to make the most of it anyway by leaning against the bottom of the tree and pretending he was a pirate.

"Help, help!" he whispered to himself. In his imagination, he'd been tied to the stern of a boat while a bunch of drunk privateers tried to have their way with him. The whispering almost took him out of his character, but it had to be done. If he shouted for help too loud, the older men would come rushing and then slap him around a bit for wasting their time. He'd learned that the hard way after pretending he was being sucked into quicksand while exploring the rainforest.

In the game, the sea was foamy and angry and he was coughing up brine while he clung desperately to the boat. "Oh, you've got to save me!" he whispered.

"We'll save you!" someone called out.

Angus opened his eyes and returned to the base of the broken tree. There was nobody around. He unclasped his hands from the invisible rope and circled the trunk.

"Oh, you're OK, then? We were worried!" the voice came again. It was a tiny voice, but loud, like someone yelling from the other side of a valley.

Angus squinted and found the source of the noise. Fluttering just above his head was a little person. A fairy? Whatever it was, it was no bigger than

Angus' hands, and his father often reminded him he had a girl's pair of hands. It hovered there looking at him thanks to a set of shimmering butterfly wins. Angus knew it was a miniature person because it had a tiny human head and could speak English. If he had stayed to look, he would have seen the little fairy person was smiling at him. He chose not to, opting instead to run screaming and crying into the settlement.

His father didn't want his sons crying, so he beat Angus long into the evening.

That night, Angus had a hard time sleeping for a few reasons. First, he'd seen a fairy. Second, his back hurt from the beating and it was tough enough to sleep on the hard ground at the best of times. Third, his brother on the other side of the tent was snoring like a pack of lions. On top of all that, after a few hours of trying to force himself unconscious, something was poking him in the belly. His brother's wayward, sleeping hand, no doubt.

Angus looked down and stared at the murky, perfect darkness before him. A flash. Another. The glimmer of wings hovering just above his gut, swooping town again and again to get his attention.

"Hello?" he whispered.

The prodding stopped. "Come outside with us, please! Please! We're sorry for the scare earlier!"

The fairy's wings glowed a soft green and fluttered toward the side of the tent. Angus was hesitant. He crawled out of the tent and followed the flapping wings a few steps before stopping.

The older men's fire was still burning and a few of the builders were hunched over on their stools, cackling and singing in a half-drunk, half-sleeping state of revelry. Angus' own father did not drink since the incident and went to sleep with the sun, but any of the other men could have spied young Angus and taken it upon themselves to dole out punishment.

"Don't worry," said the flying person, "Those men can't see you when you're with us!"

It whizzed away through the tents and unfinished buildings. Angus tried his best to follow it.

The pixie person thing led him out of the camp and into the grass. At the far end of the field, Angus could see a faint orange glow emanating from a patch of bushes. He remembered the bushes because on the first ride in he'd jumped off his cart to go pee and accidentally pricked his pecker when his father yelled at him to hurry. Since then, the older men and his brother had taken to calling him Peckerwood, and his father took the time to show him how to pee like a girl.

"Just this way! Come" the floating feller said.

There was something off about the glowing bushes, what with it being bushes that were glowing and all, but Angus couldn't exactly turn around in the dark. And besides which, if he started hollering, there was no telling what his father would do. With the only option to keep going, he jogged to an opening in the bushes, got onto his chest, and squeezed his way beneath the jagged brambles. His back ached worse than ever, and he could feel the thorns and broken edges of the branches digging into his soft flesh, tearing at his clothes, his hair, his ears. The ground was coarse and littered with pebbles, and he had visions of future conversations about his tattered pyjamas.

Sometimes things get so bad that it doesn't matter if they get worse.

Angus pushed forward. He could feel the cold air on fresh cuts and scrapes, the breeze on newly exposed skin, the rips around his knees and elbows. He found himself in an opening. And what a sight it was.

Inside the bushes was a tiny city. A dozen or more flying fairies were frolicking around glowing orbs of light. Hanging from the thicker branches and built into the ground was a network of picturesque houses. To scale cottages where more little people stood in the doorways watching Angus' amazement. The clang of otherworldly music played from somewhere deep underground. Every inch of the opening was decorated with crude wooden figures and charms made of animal teeth. It was a place that filled Angus with wonder and amazement. Even in his most vivid playtimes, he could not have concocted a place so spectacular.

The other fairies gathered around the one who had led Angus to their home. "Thank you for following me," said the fluttering one. "I am Hesiod. Will you be our friend?"

Angus covered his mouth with both of his hands. Not just to hide the smile, but to muffle the sounds of him screaming. "Yes! Of course! Oh, yes, yes, yes!" he called out.

And so, for the next month or more, Angus was their excellent friend. He told them all about the work the older men were doing and their plans for New Bethlehem. About how it was going to be the best New Bethlehem in the entire country, actually. And how all the womenfolk and the less-brave children were just champing at the proverbial bit to get there and make the town a place to be proud of. But also he told them how his father hit him at least once a day, and his brother was a giant of a man barely five years older than young Angus. He told them his secret dreams and fears, and how he'd all but regretted coming out to the encampment because the older men barely put up with him and did not hide their contempt for the, in their words, pip-squeak, peckerheaded brat.

The people of the bush told Angus secrets of their own. They revealed they were called the Qlaxci and had lived on the land since the dawn of time. Every day, they would tell Angus how much they loved him, and every day his confidence would grow just a shade larger. In the morning, he would sneak off to play with his new friends and they'd teach him their ways. As each evening crept along, he could feel his adulthood emboldening him. The older men seemed to give up directing their ire at him. His brother took to sleeping out under the stars as if to give Angus more space. Yes, something had changed.

In meeting the Qlaxci, things seemed to turn around for young Angus. And just in time, too, because it wouldn't be long before his mother and them showed up. No doubt the other children would be impressed by the man he had transformed into. They'd all stayed behind in rat infested hovels while he'd been out in the wilderness doing all the work. Every child in New Beth-lehem would see him as the big bullmoose cock of the walk in no time.

The houses were all but finished when the first chilly winds of autumn came to visit, and Angus was beyond excited to sleep indoors again. Not only would it be nice to reacquaint himself with civilised living, but the Qlaxci, for reasons they didn't explain, couldn't pass the threshold of a human house. To be sure, they were his best friends in the whole world, but the promise of a nightly reprieve pleased young Angus. The fairies would not leave him along in the tent, always trying to get him to play with them.

He couldn't tell them this after all they'd done for him. But in a lot of ways, their friendship was a hindrance. Gone were the prospects of a full night's sleep, for instance. He'd become gaunt and tired since meeting them, his puppy fat long since evaporated. A small price to pay for happiness.

A group of the older men set out one morning to inform their wives and children the town was close to completion. Angus was one of the few to remain in the town. Others stayed to stand watch, but Angus remained because he wanted his mother to see him again on his terms. It wouldn't do to have her peer into the back of a wagon and find him asleep against a sack. No. He needed to be standing tall and proud waiting for her. It would make her day seeing such a splendid young man waiting for her. What he needed to complete this reunion was a gift.

Yes, he needed to fashion together a gift of some sort, but the surrounding land wasn't a craft maker's paradise and the stores were still drawings on paper. He thought long and hard on what present he would bestow upon his beloved mother and decided to build her a Qlaxci home of her own. He set out to meet his friends for help.

"You know, as a surprise for mama," Angus explained to Hesiod. He was outlining his plans to his pixie chums about how he wanted to give something special to his mother but had limited options.

The Qlaxci conferred with each other for some time. They were worried because their houses and decorations were secret, and they didn't want to reveal their existence to outsiders. They discussed the pros and cons for an entire day, disappearing underground to hold council without Angus' prying ears. Then finally their leader, a pure white fairy called Mamlamamamama, led them back above ground to meet their human friend.

"What you have asked goes against our sacred heritage, our good friend Angus. But we love you so!"

"Yes, we love you so!" the others chanted in agreement.

"But hear me, Angus, for I have good news!"

"The best news!"

"You are invited to take part in our harvest rituals!"

"Harvest ritual!"

"If you meet with us in the forest where the river runs fastest, and the moon is at its peak, we shall give our greatest gift upon you, young Angus. This gift…"

"Oh, great and powerful gift!"

"This gift will be a most excellent surprise for your mother!"

"For the entire town, Angus!"

"They will all love this gift you will give them!"

If crying hadn't been systematically beaten out of Angus' nature by this point, he would have cried many tears of gratitude. He thanked his many friends and scampered back to his rucksack to get ready.

Angus spent the evening doing a jig around the empty room that would soon be his bedroom. When he wasn't hopping from one foot to the other, he was writing florid prose in his secret diary, so excited was he to earn a gift from his friends. There was some mystery in what it would be. Prehistoric, magical fairy people must surely be great gift givers, he reasoned.

When he could dance no more and his pencil was broken, Angus moved to the stool outside his empty home. The town looked ready to become something. A chrysalis. Rows of near-empty houses built just close enough to each other to appear neighbourly. New Bethlehem was to be commune and a promise to the rest of the country: you too can build a city in your own collective image if you select a few dozen acres of land as your own.

He had two visits before he had to reach the Qlaxci's hiding spot. First his brother came by with the fur of a felled bear. "For your room," he said to Angus with a smile and a gentle punch to his brother's shoulder. Then his brother sauntered off into the darkness in search of something else to hunt.

Second came his father, who it seemed had taken to the liquor again. He wobbled on the dust road outside their house and tried to adjust his eyes well enough to see his son. Angus said nothing. "Son," said his father, voice slurred and stumbling, like an actor who'd forgotten to read the script, "Son, I know I ain't always been fair to you, but it's how my father raised me and it's how I raised your brother too and we both seem to have turned out just fine. But... I'm sorry if I ever overstepped my bounds as your daddy, son. I mean that more than I mean much of anything. I know this don't change nothing, but I hope you know everything I've done has come from either a place of love or fear. Your mama, she's going to be here soon, with your sisters too. And I want you to know I have every intention of being the father you all deserve."

Again Angus said nothing.

"Well, son, just speaking my peace. It doesn't matter none if you don't believe me. My old man must have spun the same yarn himself a hundred times a week before he croaked. What's that they say about the pudding? Hell, we'll find out soon enough boy, but you have my word and this just might be my last word, so I hope you take it to heart. You seen your brother around any?"

Angus' voice cracked. "Out hunting."

"Again? That boy. Don't he know it's past eleven already? What's he hunting? Werewolves?"

"Dragons."

"Dragons? In this part of the world? Aw heck, son, I love you, and I'll see you bright and early."

"See you soon, pop."

Angus watched his wretched father stagger off to one of the neighbour's homes where more whiskey was available. As soon as his old man stepped into the house, Angus stood and ran off toward the woods.

Something new was pumping through his boyish veins and it took him until he reached the treeline to recognise what he was experiencing. Pride. He was proud of himself. For the longest time, the only feelings he had were the oppressive cocktail of fear and shame. But the pride? It was exhilarating. A month ago, he would have never dreamed of wandering into a midnight forest to meet magical creatures.

Carrying an empty satchel and an old lantern, it was difficult to navigate over the protruding roots and slabs of rock on the ground. He had never explored that part of the woods before, only vaguely knowing where the river led. The stream beside him trickled gently. A few insects and a solitary owl sang. Not much else besides, except his own heavy breathing and the sound of twigs breaking beneath his deliberate footsteps.

Gradually the sound of the water beside him grew louder and louder. The stream became a river when it met several other streams. There was a waterfall not too far away. Angus followed it as best he could, careful to not venture too close to the water lest it pull him in.

As he drew near to the meeting place, the animals stopped talking, replaced by what sounded like wind chimes. A hundred ornaments made of bone and bramble hung from the branches high overhead. All but the dings of the bones in the wind grew quiet. Even the waterfall seemed to shush itself. He was there.

Angus had walked into an opening in the woods. Seven massive slabs of rock stood in a circle around a small altar. The Qlaxci were dancing in a circle around the altar, the glow of their wings darker than usual. Only Hesiod broke free to join the boy.

"Ah, so nice of you to come! We were worrying!" said Hesiod.

The others said nothing.

Hesiod tugged at Angus's hand until he followed his friend up onto the altar. It was cold and moist. The boy could not get comfortable as he lay down because the altar was about half his size. He stared up at the tops of the stones surrounding him and watched with awe as his beautiful friends spun faster and faster around him, floating upward until a kaleidoscope light show of colours and shapes appeared in the sky. Angus watched this for some time in abject appreciation for a spectacle he'd earned through courage.

Something smashed through the woods nearby.

Angus snapped away from the light show above him and turned his head to face a looming shadow making its way toward him. That of friend of his, fear, the thing he'd spent all summer banishing, came back in an instant. Whatever the shadow was, it was a lumbering mess of elongated limbs, its head appeared to be carrying antlers. He looked back up at the Qlaxci for comfort, but they were gone.

He rolled off the altar and tumbled to the ground, creating a space between him and the giant figure approaching him. Part of him wanted to see what broke through the shadows and stepped into the light, but most of him wanted to escape. So escape he did. Or at least attempted. Spinning around to flee, he was one foot out of the stone circle before he felt a series of razor-like flashes at his ankles. He looked down and saw the Qlaxci diving at his feet before tearing their way into his joints with their diamond-sharp teeth.

Angus fell forward and tried to ignoring the searing, icy blasts of pain from his legs, the living things digging their way down to his bone, his tendons twisting and snapping under the pressure of a dozen or more rabid sets of teeth. He vomited, the feelings too much to contain inside him any longer. More Qlaxci were on him, smothering his back and arms, supping at his blood as he tried, with a futile, whimpering crawl, to make it back to town.

He found himself not wanting to scream, or to call out for help, or even to beg. Only one word appeared in his mind: Why?

Angus rolled over, shaking off all but the most entrenched creatures, but in doing so he saw the lurching creature was almost upon him. A human skull with bright yellow eyes looked back at him. What other features he could make out were as far from human as Angus would ever know. The Qlaxci fluttered back up overhead and sang in a language the boy could not understand. They were singing to the creature, that much he knew. His body felt limp and useless. In fact, he did not feel at all, which was to become a saving grace in the moments to come.

A stench of putrescence descended upon Angus as the creature opens its mouth revealing several rows of teeth. Out of the opened maw unfurled a snakelike tongue, which swung pendulously as it searched the aid for young Angus' scent. The creature knelt down, its giant body all but crushing Angus. Hot, sickening air escaped its nostrils. The Qlaxci were singing. Singing with all their hearts.

And then… And then…

- 58 -

... And Eights

"..."

"..."

"Now, I don't know who hurt you as a boy, but you must never, ever, tell that story again. To anyone. Please. I beg you. You can take my winnings right now if you can promise me." Joshua had turned white and seemed thankful to be sitting.

Milton said nothing. He stared down at the table, his face almost lost its blank stare for the first time since sitting down.

Alfredo laughed. "That story upset you, huh? Do dead children scare you, little man?" He dealt another hand. His knack for prestidigitation was on full display as he whirled the cards around like spinning plates. "And how does a man with no balls make it this far into the desert anyhow?"

"Don't mistake empathy of fear, sir," said Joshua.

"Yeah, just leave the man alone and deal the damn cards. You've about won, anyway. Besides which, it's not like your story was any better." Milton said. He looked over at Joshua and nodded.

All of what Milton said was true, especially the part about Alfredo winning. The man had won seven of the last nine hands, a tidbit he repeated with drunken glee to the others as often as he could. John seemed the most affected by this and had spent the last two stories gazing at the cards and at Alfredo.

The first card for each player flew across the table and landed with precision at the waiting hands of John, Joshua, and Milton. Alfredo was nodding along as he dealt. He flung out another card, and then another.

"Sonofabitch!" John called out. His hand struck out across the table like an attacking viper, and his fingers sunk into Alfredo's wrist. "You've been dealing from the bottom!"

Alfredo sneezed. "Only for me. The game was boring, so I thought I'd play one of my own. We can start from scratch if you like. I don't care. It's not like this pittance means anything."

Joshua, whose pile was smallest, shook his head. "No need for all that. You won it fair and square."

"The hell he did," John spat. "And you're just going to let him get away with this?"

Milton straightened up. "It's all just a game, champ, no reason to get testy. That said, Alfredo, you best be glad someone else caught you."

"Ha, and why is that?" Alfredo made a show of rolling his eyes.

"Because I would have shot you. Just to pass the time, you know."

Alfredo fell back in his seat with his arms to his side, exposing his chest. John stared at him through squinted eyes. A shuffling sound came from the other side of the saloon. The mayor was fishing some items out from under the counter. He reappeared from beneath it, brandishing a shotgun and a bottle of whisky.

"Pick one, lads. I don't want no trouble in this town and I don't mean to see none start neither."

John alone sat staring at the gun. The tip of his tongue appeared but for a moment and ran across his lips.

The other three pointed at the bottle.

"Just as I thought," said the mayor. He nodded and mumbled to himself as he poured each of them a fresh drink. They watched him move over to them with the speed and grace of an injured turtle. The drinks were placed before each of them, the sweet aroma of good liquor wafting upward, clearing out their sinuses as they inhaled. All four of them placed one hand on their drink and waited as the mayor made a slow retreat to his spot behind the counter.

With his free hand, Alfredo handed the cards to John, who began a one-handed shuffle.

"We need a toast," said Joshua.

"To cheating!" said Alfredo.

"To not pissing off the mayor," said John.

"To another round!" said Milton.

"Another round!" the others agreed.

They downed their drinks. Alfredo watched in amazement as Joshua sank his before even Milton. "Didn't have you pegged for a drinker," he confided.

"Oh, this? It pays to out-drink your customers."

They paused as John dealt the cards Erdnase style. Milton growled at his hand like it was an uncooperative horse.

Alfredo peeked at his cards and tossed in the ante. "I'll keep that in mind. But tell me, I'm curious: how come a salesman winds up in a remote place like this? Shouldn't you be off in some big city ripping off housewives?"

"That's my preference, for certain. I, er, was politely ordered to leave my last place of business and thought I'd try my luck on the other side of the country. I thought this desert would make for an easy shortcut. My horses disagreed." Joshua looked at the remnants of his checks and pushed half of them into the middle of the table without looking at his cards.

"You sure you ain't drunk?" Alfredo matched the bet. "What about your two? Mighty strange, all four of us winding up here by accident. What brings y'all to Genesis?"

Milton tossed in his cards. "No such thing as accidents. I'm looking for work."

"In a desert?"

"Just as good a place as any."

Alfredo nodded and then turned to John, who was still looking at his pair. "What about you, big John? How comes you wind up in a place like this?"

John paused, preoccupied with his cards and mental arithmetic. He tossed his hand in face up. He had nothing. "I'm just looking for a good place to die."

The others laughed but stifled themselves when they saw John's determined face. The man was not joking. He coughed, then dealt the flop. He was about to flip them over when Joshua whistled.

"Keep them face down, please, and deal the whole five. I want to make this interesting. If that's OK with you, Alfredo?" Joshua said. He pushed what remained of his stack into the pile and smiled at his opponent. "What was that you were saying about balls just now?"

Alfredo thumbed his upper lip and clucked. "I'm starting to like you, rich man. But just a friendly bit of advice: even if you win this hand, I can still steamroll the game. All you're doing is delaying the inevitable."

"Sometimes that is all it takes, my friend. We'll see who the last man standing is."

Alfredo nodded, struggling to hide his amusement. He chunked a stack of checks and was about to drop them into the pot when John hit the table.

"Wait," John said.

"What is it now?"

"We've all said why we're here, but you ain't. What brings you out to the desert?"

Alfredo dropped his checks one at a time into the pot as he spoke. "I'm a wanted man with dwindling options is why I'm here. But that's tomorrow's problem. Today I'm winning at poker and making some fast friends. Show 'em, rich man."

Alfredo flipped over his cards without waiting, his confidence almost tangible. He spread his hand out so everyone could see it. A full house, trips eights and a set of deuces. He leaned further back into his chair and tilted his head back while he grinned. A mottled patch of skin ran from one side of his neck to the other. "I reckon that's enough," he said.

"I think we've already covered what happens with reckoning," Joshua replied. He turned over four of his cards, each one an ace. This alone was enough to win the hand, but Joshua was not finished. Placing his palm flat against the fifth card, he slithered his fingers up and down its back until all at once there was a fifth ace looking back at them. The ace of crucifixes. "I don't think I've ever seen a five of a kind before, boys, how about that?"

John broke out in laughter. Alfredo, too, could not hide his smile. Milton nodded, stood up to reveal his stature once more, and retrieved the cards. He tossed the deck out into the desert heat and faced the mayor.

"We need a deck that isn't gimmicked and some fresh drink. One of these two magicians can pay, I'm sure."

The mayor sunk out of sight behind the bar and clambered around for another bottle. Milton returned to his seat and placed his gun on the table. He looked at his fellow travellers one by one and nodded to himself. "I'll tell you this much: at least one of us isn't who he says he is. Maybe none of us. Something is rotten, friends, and I'm not just talking about this town's residents. No offense, mayor."

"Like what?" said John.

Milton ran his fingers through his beard. "Beats the hell out of me, but I'll figure it out. Until then, how about another story?"

Avi Llio

Skinwalker

"Might as well come out and admit I've heard of this Lawman myself."
"Aw, jus' shoot me. Not another story about that weasel."
"Oh, you'll like this one. He almost to makes a difference this time around."
"Almost?"
"Ah, now, see…"

Riding his tall white horse down the trail into the valley, the Lawman could help but envision how he must appear to any onlooker. His horse's mane was flowing, glistening, free; his weapons sparkled under the high sun; he himself was an imposing figure of Justice. Yes, anyone who saw him ride by would have fallen to their knees in awe. The only thing hampering his heroic ride into town was the young Ojibwe woman who followed him at a small distance. She refused to ride on the horse with him for reasons he couldn't understand, so his ride had become a slow, plodding one. It had taken the two of them all morning to ride from nearest town to the assortments of tents without a name. Or at least no name the Lawman had bothered to learn.

The valley they were riding into was covered in fur-bedecked tipis. A tribe was on the move for some reason or another. Fires had been lit in communal areas around which natives sat and talked. As the Lawman and his majestic steed drew closer, the people gathered to watch his approach. He tried not to look directly at them as even from a distance he understood they were angry about something. The Lawman could never figure out the Comanche. They had no reason to be upset.

There was something of greater importance to attend to. The Lawman had been hired to track down a bounty for one of the neighbouring towns. A witch or perhaps an entire coven was plaguing the nearby farmers, sacrificing the livestock en masse, and even butchering the help. These were expensive things to replace. It seemed obvious to the Lawman that black magick was at play, given the severity of the murders, and so he had no problem seeking the help of tribes.

If nothing else, the Comanche had been unaffected by the witch's attack, so perhaps their self-preservation would come into play and they would help him secure his bounty. They really had a simple life with no worries to speak of, so if not self-preservation then perhaps guilt could persuade them.

The Ojibwe woman—the Lawman had taken to call her Lucy—grabbed the horse's reigns and helped guide it through the growing crowd. It was almost as if she was leading them to something.

"English?" said the Lawman. "Anyone speak English?"

He looked at pointed at various people beneath him. "How about you? Do you speak English?"

"Gophooq yusuf," said one native.

The Lawman shook his head. Did nobody speak English?

Finally, his impressive horse made its way to a tent in the middle of the settlement. It must have belonged to a chieftain or something. An old, wise man sat beside it smoking a pipe. He looked up at the Lawman and muttered something to himself.

"How?" said the Lawman.

The elder rolled his eyes, which was a regional greeting.

"Do you speak English? Nobody speaks English here."

"We all do," said the elder.

"Great!" said the Lawman, never once considering dismounting his horse. "There's a witch needs bringing to justice, and I was hoping you could help me."

"We have our own problems."

"Where? Seems like you're living the life of luxury to me. Besides, this witch is hurting the landowners around here and I'm sure it will reflect well on you if you help me."

The elder sucked on his pipe and blinked. "And just how do you propose we help you?"

"I don't know. Don't you people offer guidance or something?"

The elder sighed. "Oh, wise old man helping you on your important quest. I see. I've heard this story before."

"Yes! A spirit quest or something. If you could set me up with one of those in the next hour, I'd be most beholden to you. I'd even be prepared to give you ha—some reward money."

The elder laughed. "What we need is a little more than money. If you really want to act like you're helping us, we have—"

"Fine, half of the money."

The elder shook his head. "It's time for you to leave."

"Think of it this way, old man: helping me would put you in the good graces of your American neighbours."

"Neighbours? We didn't invite them…" the elder trailed off. He looked at the Ojibwe woman, at the Lawman who had not moved from his mount, at his people who were standing around them. He scratched the base of his neck. "You have one minute. If we can help you, we will. In return, I need a favour."

"Anything." The Lawman blinked and remained silent.

"The minute has already started."

"Ah! Well, now, here's what I've surmised so far. The witch is actually a Skinwalker. A real bad one, too. I've tracked it down to a network of caves. What I need from you people is a talisman—"

"Wait." The elder leaned forward and placed his pipe on the ground.

"Was that a minute already?"

"No. Am I to understand that's you've traipsed yourself into our home, bringing this poor girl who is not one of us along for no good reason, to ask me a Comanche about a Navajo legend?"

The Lawman nodded back at him. "That's right, yes."

The elder let out a bitter laugh that echoed through the valley. All those within earshot joined him with their own laughter. "You know nothing, sheriff, or whatever it is you claim to be. You're a fool and you're wasting our time. There's no help for you here."

The Lawman stared into the elder's eyes and smiled. Yes, there was a secret code in the old man's words, but he couldn't talk to an outsider about their myths. Such things were forbidden. But what? What was he trying to say? The laughter was key to the whole mystery. Clearly, the Lawman had found their location, but they were laughing at the idea of a Skinwalker. The actual issue was a gang of banditos who were trying to take over the region. Perhaps one landowner had put them up to it to buy up more of the land. He knew at least one such gentlemen had designed on the very valley he was sitting in, so perhaps his invisible enemy's machinations were even deeper than that. And the elder knew thanks to some ancient native mysticism, perhaps. Yes! It all made so much sense.

"Thank you, thank you, you've been very helpful," said the Lawman.

"No, thank you," said the elder. "We needed a good laugh in these dark times."

Dark times? Another clue. But there was no time to waste on such contrivances when there were bandits afoot. The Lawman turned his horse and cantered through the nest of tipis out of the valley. Laughter followed him. As did a young man.

The young man was tall and shirtless and most importantly of all was catching up with the Lawman's horse with ease. It had been the Lawman's understanding he'd received a fast horse, and not just a slightly above average one. He would have to have a talk with the stables. Slowing, he stopped to let the rider catch him. And also, by complete accident, his guide Lucy.

"Sir, I heard you down there. May I accompany you?"

"So, some of you do speak English?"

"Yes, most of us had little choice in the matter. As I was asking, though, could I accompany you?"

The Lawman spat on the ground. "I don't see why not? I must say this comes as a surprise, however. I did not think any of you people wanted to help."

"They're proud, sir, and scared too besides. But the truth is we need help, and in this new world, we must give help before they reciprocate it. Maybe if I help you, the invaders will help us in return?"

"That remains to be seen, but it wouldn't hurt. It's good to finally meet a native who talks sense."

Lucy panted nearby, gaining on the pair of horses.

"Say, what's your name, son?"

"They call me Tommy No-Buffalo."

"What an interesting name. Why?"

"Uh… because I've killed no buffalo."

"Well, neither have I, so I supposed that makes us family. You good with a bow and arrow, Tommy?"

"Sure, but I have this rifle I'm holding."

"And I'd wager you sure as shit know how to use that. Very well. You may help me. Let us ride! The cave is but two hours away as the crow flies! Ya! Ya!"

The Lawman raced off. Tommy did not move, instead calling after him. "Whoa, whoa! Sir?"

The Lawman pulled on his reins and slowed his horse. "Huh?"

"What about your wife? Is she going to walk the whole way?"

"Wife? Oh! Oh, her! No, she's not my wife. She'll catch up. And besides, it's not like she knows how to use a gun, probably. Or can she? I don't know, you probably know better than I do."

"Not really. I know nothing about her."

The Lawman sat there rubbing his earlobes and pretending to listen. He did this for three minutes. Then he opened his mouth, yawned, and said, "Right, well, anyway, let's be off!"

And off they rode.

In time they reached a place where the earth was dead, Lucy little more than a speck behind them. The place had been a victim of a long drought, with whatever had survived out there now wilted and dry to the touch. Tommy dismounted and scanned the ashen ground.

"There's an evil here," he said.

The Lawman from his vantage point surveyed the area more expertly. Ahead of them was a decline and the rocky remnants of an ancient riverbed. Something had burrowed into the rock and created a network of manmade caves. Preferably manmade. Debarked and whittled sticks had been stabbed into the ground as a warning sign and then decorated with human skulls and animal bones on the off chance the warning went unnoticed. Leading into the caves were flecks of crimsoned blood dried onto the soil, piles of broken teeth and shards of battered chests. The Lawman readied his revolver.

"No, this is all for show," he told Tommy, gesturing for him to prepare his rifle. "All that's down there are some bandits, like your father said. Don't let them get to you with these parlour tricks."

"My father?"

"Shush."

The Lawman leapt from his horse and it must have been the extended time spent sitting, because to a less generous pair of eyes it would have appeared the soldier of Justice was swaggering.

Tommy watched him following not too closely behind. He paused and felt the ground, the stakes, the bones. Nothing about the land seemed disingenuous. Shuffling along like a hunter stalking prey, he hoped the man he was following knew what he was talking about.

As they approached one of the cave mouths, they could hear the dream-like, singsong echoes of a distant conversation. It sounded like drunken conversations happening at the far side of your stately manor, which the Lawman was acutely familiar with. He put his free index finger to his mouth and entered the cave. Tommy followed. The clay intestines of the sculpted den had been made by hand, or so it seemed. Someone had dug and shaped the walls without tools. It was like being inside a homemade vase before the kiln. The walls were cold and moist and malleable.

Hanging from the top of the tunnel hung mason jars half-full of burning offal. The stench permeated the shadows better than the accompanying orange glow. Tommy looked at the floor and saw a tapestry of footprints etched there. Then he spied something far more foreboding. Three thick lines on either side of the ground leading down into the darkness. Something large had been dragged down there recently. The more he looked, the more he could see scrapes and markings in the damp clay around him.

The Lawman did not notice any of this. Instead, he mumbled something about bandits and cocked the hammer of his gun.

The tunnel grew wide and opened to a large, circular chamber. On the opposing walls were several similar tunnels, each with their own yellow-hued light for guidance. The Lawman gestured at the table in the centre of the room. It was littered with papers and maps. He ignored the cauldron heated by a green flame and filled with a bubbling, viscous liquid. Nor did he pay any mind to the small alcoves containing a menagerie of oddities. Jarred foetus, pickled heads, sacks full of belladonna, statues made of hair and bone. He looked through the papers and nodded along to the red inked handwriting.

"Seems like a wicked cave to me," says Tommy.

"Trust me, lad, I'm an expert. This is all for show. No doubt the bandits are below in their real base of operations. But they've left their plans out here, see? Now all we need to do is find them."

As if invited by the Lawman's incredulity, or perhaps the tenor of his voice, three haggard men in stained and battered clothing appeared through one of the adjoining tunnels. They looked tired, worn out, used up, shocked. The first one to enter raised his hands, the others followed suit.

"Whoa, there, ye shouldn't have come here. You best turn around before it wakes up."

Tommy was about to ask what exactly was going to wake up, but his words were drowned out by three blasts of gunfire. Each bullet exploded the space between a bandit's eyes and the three feral men fell to the floor dead. Blood and brain matter gushed out onto the walls and the floor as the gun blasts reverberated through the cavernous hive. The Lawman dropped the spent casings from his revolver, tutted, reloaded, and walked through the chamber and over the bodies.

Tommy stopped briefly to examine the dead men, but the Lawman let out a gruff snarl and he followed.

They descended deeper into the belly of the beast. The memory of the three bullets still rang through the maze of interconnected tunnels. Further underground, they could hear the shuffling of footwear and muttered instructions. There were more men. "Bobby," said one. "Quick," another, "Get the pistoles!"

The Lawman and Tommy crept through the tunnels with their weapons ready. Sounds were coming from all directions, and they could not be sure if they were hunting or hunted. A figure appeared at the junction between two tunnels and the Lawman shot it brusquely. It fell backwards and rolled down the sloping pathway, turning a corner and crashing into some unseen boxes below. Orders were barked from somewhere nearby, followed by various hushing sounds.

Something growled.

A voice called out. "Now, fellers, we don't know what you're hoping to find here, but…"

"NOW!" the Lawman yelled. He surged down the tunnel into the room below.

Tommy followed. It was a room much like the one above, but various shades of darkness. Standing at the far end of the room, a twisting, primal figure could be seen in silhouette standing before a low green fire. It writhed and transmogrified as the Lawman screamed about Justice. Tommy watched it in reverence until a bullet ricocheted around him, almost striking him dead. He stumbled backwards and took cover at the entrance to the room.

Flashes of gunfire popped from behind shadowy barricades. He fired blindly at them. Something hissed and snarled. The Lawman was laughing as he fired wildly at the bandits. They fired back, never seeming to land a hit.

"Timmy," the Lawman said, firing twice more, "Their boss is making a run for it. Head them off at the top while I deal with the rest of them."

"It ain't our blauhjhrgh," someone replied.

Tommy obliged, rushing back up the tunnelled path toward sunlight and, more importantly, away from the carnage of screams and explosions behind him.

He could hear the wheezing and pants of something not used to fleeing coming from an adjoining tunnel. As he cut through small rooms and smaller holes, he could almost glimpse the flash of a white shadow upon its escape. He pushed forward, ignoring the cramps in his muscles. Coming into the first room, a gangly grey figure was not too far ahead. Tommy fired. The figure yelped and vanished around a corner.

He reloaded and the cramps he was ignoring caught up to him. Short of breath and hesitant, he walked to where the thing had been. The floor was painted with fresh spatters of dark blood. A trail led him up the passageway and into the light. The blood trail began as little more than a few spurts, but by the time he reached the mouth of the cave it was a thick and consistent stream. He'd hurt it. All that remained was to finish the bastard off.

Except when he stepped out into the light and readjusted to the bright sun, he saw the line of blood took him not to a person but to a mangy coyote. It was limping ever slower along the dried riverbed. Tommy aimed his gun at it but relented. Just as well, as the coyote fell onto its side and began to spasm.

Someone nearby was panting.

He spun around with rifle raised to the crest above the cave. The Ojibwe woman stood hunched, hands on knees, looking down at him. She was glistening with sweat and catching her breath.

"What did I miss?" she asked.

"I don't know," Tommy answered truthfully. "If there had been a chance to figure all this out properly, it was ruined just as soon as—"

"You didn't waste any bullet on that mutt yonder?" the Lawman materialised behind him, resting his stiff hand on his shoulder.

"It's a coyote. And no."

"That's just barbaric, letting a dog like that bleed out. Oh well. Not sure what I expected from your sort. Shall we?"

"Did you catch the bandits?" Lucy asked.

"Oh, good of you to join us! And I didn't catch anyone; I shot them all dead." The Lawman holstered his revolver and clapped his hands clean before wandering off to where he had left his horse. He rode off without waiting for his two compatriots.

Tommy helped Lucy down onto the riverbed and they walked to his horse. "Why are you following him, anyway?" he asked.

"He hasn't paid me yet."

"Ah. Hop on."

They climbed onto Tommy's horse and rode together, following the Lawman. Behind them the coyote continued to convulse, coughing up bile and evil fluids as its limbs stretched and warped, its canine face returning to its human form, eyes yellow and dilated and staring off into the abyss it had narrowly avoided. It muttered ancient words to itself and to the aether as the wounds sealed themselves shut. Something resembling a laugh escaped its morphing mouth.

After some cajoling, the Lawman agreed to ride with Tommy back to his settlement. He needed to thank the elder for his clues, anyway. Their ride was quiet, and the sky was turning dark. When they came close to the valley, they could see before them clouds of thick, black smoke making their way to the heavens. Tommy stopped at the top of the hill, looking down into the valley. The tipis' smouldering remains lay flat on the ground, the livestock and several of the inhabitants were consumed by the fires. Tommy's tribe lay dead or dying in the dirt. Their lifeblood had pooled together, turning the ground a sickening red. The wails and cries were maddening.

Tommy raced on ahead and leapt off his horse, walking through the massacre with wide, disbelieving eyes. He wished he could die with his fellow man. Beneath his feet, he could feel the blood of his people, their suffering. The air stank of fire and death, and his eyes would not stop burning. Lucy and the Lawman watched him walk over the fallen. He was searching for something.

In the middle of what had been his settlement, Tommy found the elder who had been beaten to death. Laying next to him was a soldier in a green uniform. He kicked at the soldier's corpse until the Lawman stood beside him. Tommy pushed him away and fell to his knees. His words had left him, as had the only love and family he'd ever known. It was clear what had happened. With the swipe of a bureaucrat's pen, his tribe was dead. Exterminated. Perhaps for the land. Perhaps because someone considered them a nuisance. Whatever the case, it was an injustice he'd expected but never believed possible. No, things were supposed to be different. Was this the civilisation the invaders had promised?

The Lawman patted him softly on his back. "It'll be fine, son. Anyway, I have to go now. Is it OK with Lucy stays with you?"

Sudor y Sangre

"Aw hell, and I guess the Lawman couldn't have done anything about it. Damn shame."
"I don't think this Lawman is quite the hero he claims to be."
"Either way, that's grim. It hurts to think about."
"Then how about a palette cleanser? This here happened to a friend of mine down at the border. Only the assholes die in this one."
"About damn time."

O peered through the rifle's scope and looked down at the valley below. From the vantage point of the mesa, the desert looked like spice seller's cart, an endless stretch of paprika and chilli, sprinkled with coarse green herbs. O's thoughts often turned to food because there was none out there. The hares were skittish, and the coyotes were sly.

It was not an ordinary creature O was hunting, however. No living being had those tracks nor left its prey unblemished and exsanguinated. The nameless creature was down there in the vast emptiness. Close by and hungry.

O moved the scope and searched for movement. A fox cub searched for its den. Dried out cactus blanched in the sun. Three wild horses trotted around a dark slab of rock. They were free and enamoured with the brittle, saline remains of the plant life. The horses. O would use the horses.

The creature had proven elusive, more so than any other beast O had tracked. Only its insatiable appetite for blood drew it out. A bleeding horse—the white one seemed the most likely to gush—would be too hard to ignore in a realm where the only other option was a slow, protracted death.

That was the plan, then: ride down the scraggly rim of the mesa; ride down the white horse; tie it to… something; wait downwind with rifle in hand until the bountiful meal proved too much to ignore. But what of the other predators? Scavengers? A second meal site closer to O's next perch. No. The creature O was hunting was cruel enough to sink its fangs into an injured, frightened horse, but no other carnivore in the desert would get close until it was dead.

Except for O.

They rode down as best they could to where the horses trotted when the three of them broke. A gunshot followed by a scream. A prolonged scream that carried across the entire desert floor and ricocheted off the mesa. Some, O keenly observed, were in distress.

Through the scope, O could not make out anything. There were no further screams. The fading memories of the bullet's echo still rattled through the air, but beyond that…

Some distance away, beyond the patch of rocks that had so fascinated the now-vanished horses, was a small stream of black smoke. How had they missed that earlier? Something had burnt through the night. O cantered toward it, rifle at the ready, eyes trained on the motionlessness of the desert. Any movement at all and O would fling their rifle toward it.

A buzzard sat pecking at something buried in a patch of brittlebush. There was a trail of blood leading to the shrubbery and a leather boot protruding from it. O left the animal to its meal and followed the trail. The black smoke and the dark line of spilt blood seemed to meet just beyond an incline. O rode on.

The raised ground was the edge of a dried riverbed. Down not too far below was the charred remains of a wagon laying on its side. Three bodies lay face down in the dirt, coagulated crimson sludge pooled around what remained of their heads. Each of the corpses wore a near-identical outfit, a uniform. Private security. Their guns were still in their hands.

Nearby, someone was sobbing.

It was a woman in what had been a white dress. She lay caked in riverbed slime and hidden between two boulders. Her hair was matted with grime, face fading, tired, spent, eyes red. Skin red, too. Blotches of water were pooling on her freckled, burnt skin. When she saw O, she screamed again.

O took a spare canteen from their waist and tossed it at the woman's feet. "¿Estás bien?"

"Stay away from me, you damned Spaniard, ain't you did enough?" she hollered.

"Drink. Are you OK?"

The woman uncapped the canteen and gulped greedily with no thought of the hours to come. Satisfied, or as satisfied as she could be, she hurled the empty canteen back at O. "Do I look OK, mister? All my pa's men are dead. Just finish me off and kill me before you have your way with me. That's why you came back, ain't it? You filthy pig. Go on then. Do it."

O appreciated the woman's spirit. "I am not who you are thinking I am, lady. Climb on. I will take you home."

The woman peaked over the rim of the boulders and gazed at her fallen protectors. Straining to find her feet, she stood hunched and exhausted. She patted the warhorse's face. "Big horse."

"The biggest."

"What's his name?"

"Pequod."

"Help me up, then," the woman said, tugging at O's arm and climbing onto the back of the saddle. "Silly name for a horse this size. You shoulda called it Ajax."

"Next time."

From her new position, the woman looked sorrowfully at the dead men. "They ain't getting no funeral, is they? Mind if I say a few words? It's all they're gonna get out here."

"Por supuesto. Go ahead."

The woman delivered a eulogy as dry and as barren as the land surrounding them. If she had ever known, much less loved the dead men, she was hiding it well. She then pointed in the vague direction of where her home was, and then they were on the way.

The woman did not look back once at the corpses, but O turned once or twice to look for their prey. It was out there. Closer than it ever had been. And it would remain so.

The woman was Cordelia. She lived in the town across the border and was the heir of a tobacco fortune. Her father, she said, was an ass hair away from being a senator. Cordelia and her convoy had planned to take her to Pueblo de Mentiras to marry a local tycoon. O knew him well. He was a bastard, a son of a thousand bastards. Their marriage was to be one of convenience, although for whom remained to be seen.

"And that's when it happened," Cordelia continued. "We camped for the night and I guess some banditos or something showed up. They started shooting. I hid. My father's men all died. They set the wagon on fire and I guess just assumed I was in there."

"Did they say anything?"

"What sort of question is that? Ain't you supposed to offer condolences when someone tells you a sad story?"

"Sorry. Did they say anything?"

"I think so. Probably Spanish."

"Then perhaps the man from Mentiras got cold feet? Someone didn't want you getting married."

"Aw, that's a stretch. It was just regular bandits."

"At night? In the middle of this desert? And they knew exactly where you were?"

"Who else could it have been?"

The two of them rode onward through the haze, the horizon marked with mammoth stone slabs. Cordelia sat talking for several hours, only pausing to beg for another swallow of O's canteen. It was the edge of dusk when she prodded O, as if woken from a dream, and said, "I'm hungry."

O nodded but continued to ride.

"You ain't hear me? I said I'm hungry."

"I heard."

Cordelia returned to talking to herself for another fifty trots before O swung their rifle to a nine o'clock position and fired once.

"What the hell are you doing, boy?" Cordelia asked.

O did not reply, instead jumping off the horse and walking in the direction they'd fired. Cordelia watched as her rescuer drew a knife from their boot and walked to a small clump of aloe. O crouched, their back to Cordelia, and lingered there for several moments. Cordelia was so confused she was quiet for the first time since mounting Pequod.

O stood and spun around. Face decorated with a handsome smile. What they were holding was not so handsome. A skinned rabbit in one hand and the blade and the bloodied hair of the felled animal in the other.

"Not eating that," Cordelia said.

Nodding once again, O wrapped the skin in a thick sheet of wax paper and then placed it in a satchel. They strung the meat's hind legs together and hung it from the saddle. Cordelia tried to push it away from her filthy dress. Before returning to the saddle, O fondled the inside of the satchel and retrieved a stiff piece of hard bread. Cordelia accepted it as one might accept an invitation to a hated relative's funeral. She rad there, tottering on the horse as they rode on, contemplating how hungry she would have to be before she sunk her teeth into the meal. It was not a long internal debate. Before five minutes passed, she was nibbling on the edges of the bread. It was tough and tasteless, much like her father. Much like O. Much like the desert itself.

When the bread was eaten and Cordelia once again had use for her mouth, she nudged O. "Hey, so, enough about me, how come you were out here in the desert in the first place? Awful big place to get lost in."

"Hunting."

"For what? There's nothing out here worth eating."

"A legend."

"Oh. I see." She did not. "Sorry for taking you away from your hunt, I guess. My daddy will reward you real generous when we get home, just you watch."

O shrugged. O and the legend were destined to meet. Some things are unalterable, especially by human hands.

By the time the sun was little more than the orange tilt at edge of a purple sky, it was clear they would have to stop for the night. The town was still two days ride away. They stopped beneath an arched slab of rock, a giant sandstone doorway. O built a fire on an elevated chunk of rock and rolled out a sleeping bag for Cordelia. It took her some convincing to get down from the horse, more still that it was safe to sleep there. O cooked the rabbit and boiled the dregs of water to make a mug of hot cocoa. Cordelia played with the sinewy tendons of the rabbit's leg, her teeth strumming it tentatively like a novice guitarist, but she did not eat, waiting instead for O to offer the hot cocoa.

In time, Cordelia gave in to her exhaustion and lay flailing in place. O leaned back against the pillar of rock and watched the skies until they could watch no more.

Somewhere the legend was watching them.

Somewhere hunters far more malicious than any mythical beast were resting in a camp all their own.

Sunrise came fast in the wilderness. Cordelia woke to discover O had already prepared a small breakfast of oats and barley. Fresh-brewed coffee sat steaming in a metal mug. The satchels were already beginning to sag.

"First thing we need to do is refill our bottles."

"Out here?"

"If possible."

They ate and then rode on, Cordelia holding O tighter than the day before. The earth beneath them was whiter than it had been, the plants sparser than they had been, animals all hidden underground except for the bleached remnants of those who couldn't make it. To the east, the ground was making a steady rise to a chain of hills, to the north a bushy green dollop of something. Trees? That was the hope.

"Say, how come you didn't ride the way my guards did? There was a trail and everything."

"Your guards a dead. Their killers are still out here. I thought this way would keep us away from them."

"And by 'thought' you mean what?"

"We're being followed."

That they were. To the southeast and making no pretence about it, three dark riders were gaining on them. They galloped forward at an almost leisurely pace. Their mounts were strong and thoroughbred, well fed, and moved like the military had trained them. Cordelia looked back and screamed. It almost sounded as if the strangers laughed in return.

"That's them! They's the ones what shot my daddy's men!"

"Hold on."

Taking their spurs to Pequod, O broke off into a mad sprint. A single rifle shot cracked behind them. A warning shot. Cordelia wrapped her arms around her saviour and looked back. A trail of dust rose from the ground and consumed the air behind their pursuers. The three men whooped and hollered as they let off extra rounds. If they caught them, as it seemed they must, they would take their time with Cordelia. Of that much she was certain.

The green growth in the distance grew as O raced on. Pequod's speed grew the further it ran. Cordelia watched the riders behind them shrink as their own speed tapered off long before the great warhorse's did. The hunters were no longer shooting at the heavens, but at the fugitives. The ground exploded into plumes of grit and dust as O slowed.

An oasis. A handful of trees, a pool of cold water, a shack.

"Hide!" O gestured at the shack.

Cordelia all but fell off Pequod as she ran to the decrepit structure and pressed herself to the ground, hoping in vain it would swallow her until the hunters either died or went elsewhere.

O turned Pequod to face their pursuers and rode headfirst toward them, leaping off at the last moment. As they approached, they scattered to avoid the charging horse and O fired a single shot. The dome of the first hunter's head exploded, and he flipped backward off his horse. O rolled to another position in the shallows of the pool and aimed at the second rider. His chest tore open as he rode forward and his body somersaulted to one side, slumping to the ground.

The third rider turned and fled. O hurried to reload. Taking aim, the rider was half hidden by the low sun and all O could do was send a bullet to kiss the man's arm. He yelped and cried and disappeared into the desert.

O was quick to check on the two fallen hunters. The one with the cavernous chest was still clinging to air but could not form words in his blood-filled mouth. American. No credentials, nothing on him but guns and water, but American all the same. It was obvious in the attire, the complexion, the mewling death. The other corpse told the same story.

Collecting the goods and depositing them beside the near-catatonic Cordelia, O was fast to usher the hunters' horses to the pool. They waited there, loyal only to the living, as O walked to Pequod. Resting a hand on the horse's face, O whispered with a rare adoration. "Buena, buena. Eres hermosa. Ti amo. Shh shh."

O removed the saddle and satchels and dropped them, wiping down Pequod's strong back with the attentiveness of a doting parent. The horse whinnied and lapped at the shallow waters as O hoisted the first corpse up onto it.

Cordelia lingered in her hiding spot, watching her rescuer position the bodies on the back of the magnificent horse. She watched, puzzled, as O bound the deceased to each other and to the horse. The confusion only grew when O kissed and whisper to the steed. With one last loving stare, O backed away from Pequod and struck it once, twice in its hind. It seemed to understand. Running away from the oasis.

Cordelia did not understand. "Hey, that's our horse!" She walked out of the shack and stood beside O.

"No. It is my horse. The man who got away might track it instead of us. It will buy us some time. Can you ride?"

"Sure I can. I can shoot a gun, too, since you're asking."

O tossed Cordelia a spare pistol. "Nice of you to tell me now. Get some rest. We will ride when the sun sets."

They set up in the cramped shack and tried to sleep. The horses tugged at their ropes outside, full of water and eager to move on. O slept in a dreamless stiffness reserved for the exhausted and the mournful. Cordelia could not sleep, instead speculating on who had built the shack where they had gone, and who had hired the men to kill her. Through the grogginess found between realms of consciousness, O would wake every five minutes to the sounds of her rhetoric, of aimless shuffling, of worn heels against ancient planks.

In time the noise became a comfort and its absence that woke O up for good. They lay there facing the wall with an oppressive, looming silence devouring the room. Someone or something was stalking the cramped space of the fetid room.

Cordelia. Her hand pressed against O's hips, her lips forming a soft suction cup on the base of O's neck. "I never thanked you for saving me," Cordelia whispered. O didn't move, preferring to let the actions take their own course.

"Oh, thank you, thank you," Cordelia whispered. Lips frantic, inexperienced, hands exploratory and distracted, moving from waist to belt to buttons to waist. After a lingering silence, a cold tiny hand slid beneath O's jeans. It hovered there for a moment. Then recoiled.

"You're a woman!?"

They spent the waning sunlit hours in silence, O watching the sky turn a deep picotee blue; Cordelia lost in her self- imposed embarrassment. With little more than the waxen light of the gibbous moon, O gathered their supplies and fastened them to the waiting horses. It was growing cold and there would be no fire on the ride. O took a blanket made of doe skin from a bag and handed it to Cordelia.

"Desert nights are unforgiving. I'm sure you already learned this."

Cordelia said nothing.

They rode in silence through the desert. Their perimeter remained illuminated by the moon, but the horizon on all sides was dark and treacherous. Shapes morphed; shadows promised great rock titans only to yield nothing. Faint green shimmers of animal eyes reflecting the indifferent satellite above them.

Something howled. The howl was like nothing Cordelia had heard before, and yet she maintained her fresh vow of silence. O had heard the howl only once. Weeks earlier. It was not something worth breaking the muted ride over. At least not yet.

In the early morning, the first false promises of daybreak presented themselves and Cordelia found her voice. "So, you're a woman."

"No."

"But you have—"

"I am what makes me happiest."

"Are you saying you're a man?"

"No."

"Then what?"

"It doesn't matter."

Cordelia looked down at the loose rocks. Small growths of vegetation were forming in the broken earth. "Were you raped as a kid or something? Did something bad happen to you? Is that why you lead young women on insinuating you're a man?"

O laughed. "You seem to be a little preoccupied with rape. Maybe you should dwell on that instead of worrying about me."

"So you don't deny you led me on?"

"We've been riding two nights now and you don't even know my name. Besides, you were the one to do all the touching."

"I guess there were a lot of things I didn't know about you. But you must have been felt up by an uncle or your mother hit you or your daddy hated you. Something must have gone wrong in your brain."

"Wrong? I'm happy. Maybe where you come from everything starts with trauma, but I had a good childhood. I am still close with my family. This is just how I prefer to live. It feels closer to who I am inside."

"I don't understand."

"It's a good thing you don't have to."

They returned to silence. Just as well too, as not too far behind them another set of hooves kicked up loose rocks. O turned. Silhouetted by the lightening sky were five swaying figures. Large men on larger horses, sauntering as if they were running errands, rode not too far behind them. If they could not see the two of them in the pre-dawn dimness, it was only a question of time before the sun corrected its mistake.

"Hey," said O.

Cordelia didn't answer. Riding a little faster to get ahead from O.

"Don't make any noise, idiota," O whispered with a hiss. "There's five men behind us. I don't think they see us yet."

"WH—"

O tossed some water from their flask and splashed Cordelia. "I said no noise. Tonta."

They had to think fast, and Cordelia was no help, flailing with her reigns in a confused attempt at speeding off. The land offered no suggestions either. It had been miles and hours since O last surveyed the land, and all they could see in that moment was shadows and the ragged outer rim of a faraway canyon.

"Hey," Cordelia tried to whisper. It was not her forte. She pointed at the dark shape of a tree. "That's Devil's tree."

"Yes, and?"

"And that means we're close to Devil's Gorge."

"Oh." They'd made it a lot further than O had expected.

O rode in that direction. "If they follow us down there, we'll know they're bad."

"Mm-hm," even in the darkness, O could feel Cordelia's pleased-as-punch grin. "And they'll have to ride single file too. At least until they reach Devil's Gulch. Low-water season."

O was impressed. "I'm impressed," they said. "We can get off the horses halfway down and hide."

"Ooh!" Cordelia caught herself, slapped her hands against her mouth. "We can use Devil's Cave for cover. It's about halfway down."

O wanted to ask about who'd come up with the naming scheme for the place. The Anglos sure had a way with words. No doubt they'd come up with it after murdering a village and stealing all their alcohol. Speaking, though, would be a mistake. The shadows behind them were making murmurs of their own, their gruff voices carried by the wind. Hard syllables stabbed at O's ears.

The twosome rode into the gorge and followed the narrow trail into the depths of the canyon. Above them, the sky was lighting up. Behind them, the riders were debating their approach, their words travelled into the gulch. Americans, for sure. Cordelia lifted her head, recognising one voice, and almost yelled back at it. Her eyes glazed over with the tears of betrayal and her head shook. Specific Americans, then.

They reached the cave and slipped off the horses. Cordelia landed on the ground with surprising aplomb. The two horses rode on without instruction. Inside of the cave was not much to speak of. It was closer to a cupboard than a cave, except for the small burrow leading deep into the earth on the back wall. O and Cordelia pressed against opposite walls and listened, both grasping their weapons, ready to ambush the not-so-strangers. Cordelia, especially, had death in her eyes. O could only watch as the woman struggled to suppress sudden urges for violence.

"Dammit, dammit, god," she was whispering to herself, stopping only when the first rider seemed close.

"Who's the guy helping her, then?" one rider asked.

"Beats the hell out of me. She was supposed to be dead two nights ago."

"'Supposed to'? I thought you said you shot here."

"We left her in a burning carriage. Seemed good enough for me."

"You dipshit, Charlie. You absolute cretin. Going to be a lot harder to pin this on the Mexicans this close to home. You buffoon. You degenerate fucking knave."

"Easy, Jim-Bob. Nothing's changed. We're still going to get out war."

Cordelia clenched her teeth and let out a pained sound. Spit flew down onto the floor. "Jim-Bob, you sonofabitch."

O, wide-eyed and concerned, shook their hands, their head. The riders had almost reached them and came to an abrupt stop.

"What was that?" said Jim-Bob.

"Dunno," said one of the others. "That cave there?"

"Ah, she can't be that stupid."

Two men leapt off their horses and unholstered their weapons. Cordelia was ready. O not so much. They'd noticed something moving in the burrow. A long, insectoid limb with feline claws was scraping at the ground. Then another limb. It stunk of gunpowder, whatever it was, and it was forcing its way out of the hole.

"Uh, hey," O whispered.

"Guns ready!" a voice said from outside.

"Uh, oh no," O whispered, swatting at Cordelia's waist.

"I'll kill him," said Cordelia.

"Can't kill all five of us, little miss. We've got the drop on you now. Should have kept riding. Not that your daddy would have cared much to see you. You and your boyfriend best toss out your guns now."

"Actually—"

"This is not the time for that," said O. "Do as they say. But don't leave the cave."

"Ekk-ekkk-ekkk-sszzzfrrrpekekeke," said the thing in the burrow. Its head protruded from the hole. Bulbous bug eyes and a spiral tongue attached to what could have been a coyote's head in another life. Cordelia had yet to notice.

O tossed out the rifle.

"That's all we got."

"But I can't leave the cave," added Cordelia. "Got my foot trapped."

Jim-Bob and the others laughed. "What a stupid bitch," said Jim-Bob to more laughter. "Alright, baby girl, I'll help you get out of a hole for a change."

"That don't even make sense, Jim-Bob, you sack of shit."

"Hey, I'm not the one with my leg trapped in a cave. You should have burnt in the carriage like a good little girl."

They could hear breathing like an asthmatic sprinter as he walked to the mouth of the cave. He poked his head in. He stunk of rotten teeth, which was almost enough to hide the stench of the creature in the hole. His dim eyes looked Cordelia then O up and down, then glimpsed the thing coming out of the hole in the wall.

"Friend of yours," he said before the creature hissed and leapt at him, stabbing its unwound tongue into the side of his next. He fired into the cave and staggered backward, tumbling down the narrow trail as the other four men opened fire.

"What the hell was that?"

"I'll tell you in a minute," said O. "They're reloading."

Cordelia smiled and rolled out of the cave, giving O just enough time to roll out and retrieve their rifle before opening fire. She picked off three of the riders with succinct accuracy while O levelled the fourth just as they were about to return fire. The men fell from their horses. The horses, free from their masters, turned and fled back up the narrow path.

"I told you I could shoot!" said Cordelia. Her pride was tangible. She looked down the slope at the limp, pale body of Jim-Bob. The creature was gone and so was all the man's blood. "Now, what the hell is that thing."

"It doesn't have a name yet. I call it the Chupacabra, though."

"That's a stupid name."

"Oh, is it? Come. It can't be far."

"We should call it a Devil Dog or a Devil Coyote or something."

O was not listening, checking the fallen Jim-Bob for any clues instead. The animal had left sprinkles of blood along the white grit of the trail leading down into the gulch itself. O walked alone along the line and down into the bottom of the trail. The riverbed waiting was all shallow, coarse sand and sedimentary rocks piled up along the floor. Splashing along down the winding embankment was the Chupacabra itself. In the ever-growing light of the dawn, the creature seemed confused, frightened even. It continuously spun its head, massive black eyes unblinking but afraid, tongue ready to strike at some unseen threat.

O crouched and looked down the barrel of their rifle.

"You're not going to kill it," said Cordelia.

"I'm a hunter. I've been tracking this thing since I was a child."

"And you tracked it. Good job. But we're out in the middle of the desert and I've got nowhere to go. Look at it. Look at that thing. It's no threat to you. In fact, I'd say it saved our asses just now."

"I'm a hunter."

"Big deal. You want to define yourself by your own terms so bad, here's your chance."

O squinted and looked at the creature. It was swiping at the sky, blinded by the light. O looked over at Cordelia. She didn't look like the person O had met not too long ago.

Visitor

"Hey, you can't just keep ending your stories all abrupt like that. It's not as smart as you think it is."
"Check. Who says?"
"Says me. Fold. Says me, buddy. But since we're playing it like that…"

A heavy, uneven set of boots hammered down over the floor, hands idly rattling the bars of every cell along the corridor. They stopped outside of hers. She didn't want to turn around. Didn't need to. There was only one man who ever came to visit, and he always said the same thing. She could hear him deliver a rehearsed cough, which was another thing he always did. Then he said the thing he'd been saying for a week.

"You know, Eleanor, we're going to hang you regardless, so you might as well cleanse that soul of yours and confess your crimes."

"I have nothing to confess."

"That poor family. We can't give those children a proper funeral, you know. What did you do with the bodies? Eat 'em? Did you eat those poor, innocent children?" He spat the next words like they were too sour for his mouth, "Did you, witch?"

"Something took them."

"Right. We're still on that nonsense? Green lights and earthquakes? The court won't believe those lies, and if you think they will, you're a bigger fool than I thought. And then there's the matter of the other prisoners…" He trailed off, gesturing at the other cells. All empty. They'd been full a week ago.

"You can't pin that on me. These conditions would kill just about anyone."

"Even so. What court will protect you?"

"Any fair trail would see this is all circumstances is all. I'm a victim just as much as those people."

The man gripped the bars and pressed his face between them. "Except, here's my secret: there ain't gonna be no trial, because we both know you did it. I'm not wasting the judge's time with a…"

"Can't even stomach the word, huh? But what justice is that? Killing me out back like an old dog."

"It's more justice than you showed that sweet, blessed family, that much is for certain."

"I didn't kill no families. You have no weapons, no motives, no witnesses. No damn proof."

"We found you out there hiding in their cupboard."

"Exactly! Are you suggesting a delicate little flower such as myself committed the perfect, clueless crimes and then instead of escaping waited around in a cupboard? Just think how foolish you've been sounding this past week. I implore you. It's been fun and all, wasting away down here, having our little meetings, but just think about how little sense you're making. If I killed them, all I'd have had to do was go home, right? I'd have gotten away with it. So why? Why did I hide in that cupboard?"

He'd stopped listening a long time ago, instead wiping the silt from the higher edges of the bars. "Foolish? You're going to be dancing like the court fool at the end of my rope by the end of the week. Why not save yourself a few more sleepless nights and just confess? It's that simple. I will set you free."

She turned in her cot and stared at the damp wall. "This has gotten asinine. You are asinine. Either bring the judge or the priest one next time. Hell, bring the town drunk. I bet his conversations would make more sense. You have cheese where your brains should be, sir."

He laughed the way cuckolds do, almost giving into his base desires and opening her cell door. Eleanor, with her back to him, could feel him tremble against the iron bars. But he was not the type of man to strike a woman while she was awake. "I will enjoy watching you die, jezebel," he said before stamping out of the jail as he had six times before.

She rolled over onto her back and looked up at the ceiling. Black spots were growing between the plastered cracks up there. Damp, green patches were blossoming every hour as the something leaked from the world above. In the old days, they would have burnt a rotten house down. Now they seemed intent on letting the disease spread. No wonder the other prisoners died.

Not just the jail needed to be burnt away. The entire town needed to be cleansed with a healing fire. Damn, she thought, I'm sounding like that dick. Her entire life she had lived in peace. Not once had she so much as raised her voice. And yet here she was. The only prisoner in a forsaken town. Nobody seemed to care. There was no outrage at her arrest.

In the evenings, after the angry man left, she would look over to the other cells and pray for a drunk or someone else from elsewhere to be brought in. Nobody. Just the man. He said he was the assistant mayor. It was always those with the smallest taste of power who would flaunt it most violently, without finesse or centuries of inbred posturing behind them.

She couldn't blame them entirely for suspecting her. She had been there at the ranch. But she knew she hadn't murdered the family. She should have run when she had the chance. Those words. Truly the worst words in the language: should have. Visit anywhere with alcohol and you'll find a dozen men drinking themselves dead with those words in their mouths. Should have. Should have.

Because, ultimately, she didn't run. At the time, she was terrified and interested only in surviving another night. When she closed her eyes her lids still glowed with the sickly green light that had consumed the forest. Then there was the screaming. The child rattling the handle of the cupboard. Pleading. The aftermath. All the other prisoners dying. Her only source of company being the nightmares and a man on the outskirts of the vicinity of power. She didn't even know his name. Didn't even know who the family were, truth be told.

And not a damn one of her friends came to visit.

The following morning, or at least what could have been the following morning, a man sat on a stool outside her cell waiting for her to wake up. A different man. He was dressed like a priest but was not from the town's church. Eleanor jolted upright and gawked at him. A tray of grains and a cup of old milk and spit waited for her next to the bars, but for the first time in a while she ignored them to focus on her unknown visitor. Was she smiling? Blushing?

"Why, hello there," she said, trying to sound as cheery as she could.

"Ms Taft, do you know who I am?" She did not. "I am Father Pierce Bolton from the capital."

"Oh, finally, someone with some sense. Now—"

"Quite. This isn't the first time we…" he looked down at his shoes. "Wouldn't you like the families of the deceased to have some closure? I will move you to the city if you can at least lead us to the bodies. Might protect that neck of yours, at least. I can't promise freedom, but a reprieve from execution at least. You'll have ample time to save your poor soul."

"I didn't kill no one."

"I believe you believe that to be true. But the facts stand, and there are no other explanations. No suspects, nor information. Nothing. If it wasn't you, then who?"

"It were those demons! I told them everything when they brought me in here. I saw them. These otherworldly grey demons took the family away."

"We agree, at least, that demons were involved. But tell me: how come you were there at all? What was your business being out at a private ranch?"

"I… it's just how it played out. Running errands in them parts. I told the other guy, I'm a victim of circumstances."

The priest leaned forward and did his best to appear intimidating. It worked as well as expected. The man had spent too many years in city churches ignoring the needs of the civilians. He was unaware of how he looked, however, and seemed to think he was scaring Eleanor. "You're going to take me to where those poor souls are hidden, lady. This town has been very patient with you, and I must insist you give them the peace they deserve."

Eleanor resisted the impulse to immediately say no. A plan was forming in her mind, prompted by the suggestion she return to where the family died. She bit the inside of her bottom lip until the urge to smirk subsided. "I will take you to where I last saw them. Whether their bodies are there is anyone's guess. Just you, me, a deputy, and the man who keeps visiting me."

"You don't get to make demands."

"Or what? You'll hang me? Those are my term. Otherwise, if my breakfast stays there any longer, it may start tasting good."

The priest was an actor. He did what he could to look lost in thought. "We will consider it. I will let you know soon. Until then, please know I will pray for you."

"I'll be here, Pierce," Eleanor said. With a laugh? Why was she laughing? There was no good reason. Although, after a few days in jail, a person will find any excuse they can to laugh. The priest wasn't amused. He left the room, shaking his head and counting his beads.

Eleanor blinked up at the invading spores on the ceiling. She didn't have much time to plan her defence, nor did she know what they would find waiting for them at the ranch. The only thing she was confident about was she would not be spending much longer behind bars. She stood and closed her eyes. Standing on her tiptoes, she imagined herself in a vast expanse and spun around enjoying her fictitious freedom.

The following morning, or at least what could have been the following morning, a deputy she'd never seen before stood at her door with a change of clothes and three stern words. Eleanor did as she was told, aware of the man's eyes as she slid into the starched uniform. He handcuffed her, and she followed him upstairs. There were seven people waiting for her outside the jail, which was a lot more than they'd agreed upon. She'd agreed? Hadn't she? Besides the deputy, the mayor's assistant, and the priest, there were four new strangers. A medicine woman in a white outfit stood carrying a satchel full of jars and bandages. Then there was a man with a pencil and a pad of paper, whose wool suit revealed everything Eleanor needed to know about him. In addition, two porters stood to the side, carrying an excess of baggage and looks of mild contempt.

"Who are these people?" Eleanor asked.

"Witnesses, a journalist, medical assistance should we need it. The mayor and the sheriff both gave this the go ahead. Remember that you could have just drawn a map, and we'd already be on our way to the city," the priest replied. He'd been practicing his lines.

"It's a long way to their residence, and it's the middle of august. Are you sure you want all these people cramped together heading that way?"

"You murdered an entire family in cold blood," the mayor's assistant spat. "I think we need all the bodies we can muster."

"Oof. 'Bodies'? Poor choice of words there. Shall we?"

Eleanor walked down the road toward where she thought the ranch was. It was a good few miles out of town, around the other side of a mountain. She enjoyed an entire minute to herself before she heard whistles and yells behind her. Eleanor turned, smiled, and tried to slap her forehead, the tight cuffs reminding her that this was impossible.

The ride was as cramped and as bumpy as Eleanor expected. The air in the wagon smelled of sweat and sour breath. Outside was not much better. A porter and the deputy rode up front, the other porter sat on the back of the roof. Every few minutes the mounted porter's buttocks would slap the top of the stagecoach.

Inside, the medicine woman had fallen ill with the stench and was hanging her head out of an open window. The priest and the mayor's friend were sleeping, arms crossed, heads pressed into the corners at odd angles. The only company Eleanor had was the journalist who had realised too late their suit was out of season. Its brown fabric was growing darker by the moment. Eleanor grinned at him. He looked over at the sleeping accusers and the nauseous woman like a guilty conspirator. He leaned in and smiled back.

"Now, I am supposed to be impartial in all this," he whispered, "But I want you to know I believe you played no part in this tragedy."

"That means a lot."

"This isn't the first time a family has gone missing from a ranch. They were vague when I talked to them. Can you tell me what you saw when they disappeared?"

"Ain't you read the reports? I don't know if I can make it any more believable than I already did. Bright lights, demons, you know, the usual stuff."

"I only read censored copies of the report. Who were these demons? What did they look like?"

"Like nothing I've ever seen before. Tall and naked and they stunk like old piss."

The journalist checked in with the sleepers before he slid a sketch out of his notepad. He showed it to her. A few details were off, but she recognised them instantly. She nodded. The journalist nodded. The sheet disappeared back into the notepad.

Without moving from his hunched position, the mayor's colleague sighed. "I hope you're not buying into her humbug about spooky sky people and flashing lights in the sky."

"Actually, sir, I've been reading up on similar reports across the frontier. This would be the seventh vanishing to occur under similar circumstances. They killed the last witness too."

"Horseshit. This crazy bitch killed them and ate them. Open and shut case. We should go through her stools at the prison looking for fingernails, not wasting time up here. You say there were other towns? I say she killed them and at them too. She looks like the running type. Bet the only reason she don't have warts is she don't stay in one place long enough."

"I have warts. I caught them off your mother."

"We should just find the nearest tree and leave you there." The assistant closed his eyes and snored.

The journalist broke his gaze and retreated to his notes, ignoring Eleanor for the rest of the ride.

"Blurgh," said the medicine woman.

They arrived at the ranch a little after noon, or at least it seemed to be a little after noon. It was easy to see why the family had fought so hard for the location. A little pocket of paradise hidden between mountains and forests. The ranch itself was surrounded by honey yellow fields, quickly overgrowing now that the animals were gone. Surrounding the fields were the trees, which literally went on for days in two directions. In happier times, it would have been a fun place to paint.

Clouds, though, as if summoned to ruin any illusion of handsomeness, gathered above them with the vague promise of an awful night to come.

The journalist was the first to leave the wagon. He walked five paces, then stopped to take in the air and survey the surrounding land. Or at least he tried. The medicine woman surged past him, projectile vomiting as she did so, and rushed to the nearby outhouse. They all did their best to ignore her sounds.

The two porters held onto their noses while trying to unload the baggage.

"We don't have time for that. I don't know why you all insisted on bringing so much," the deputy said.

"We have all the time in the world, deputy," the assistant said. "Keep unloading it all."

"There's a storm coming… associate," the deputy muttered. He wasn't interested enough to argue. "Let's just get what we came for from this lady so we can all get back to town before the roads flood. Trust me when I say you don't want to be caught out here with your pants down."

"Pants down? Just what exactly did we come here to do?" Eleanor asked. "But I agree. I last saw the family about a half mile that way. In the woods. I'd point but," she rattled her chains.

The priest nodded. "Then it is decided. Have the men stay here with the… indisposed. The sooner this is all resolved, the sooner God can have his justice."

The assistant pointed at a tree. A rope was already fastened to it. Before they disappeared, the family had taken it in turns to swing on it. Perhaps it was Eleanor's turn. "That tree right there will get justice taken care of right quick. No one back in town would question it."

"Pretty sure I'd have a thing or two to say about it," said the journalist.

"Yes, and I'm sure the church would have an issue with it. You can't just go around hanging folk," the priest added.

"You guys do it all the time."

The debate on the efficacy of hanging continued as the five of them left the porters and the medicine woman to drop their respective luggage.

They walked in single file across the grass and through the woods. The deputy took the rear, rifle ready, eyes wide and alert. Eleanor took point, almost skipping through the wet earth toward the scene of the (alleged) crime. She had missed nature and wished only that she were barefoot so she could enjoy the touch of the mud between her toes. Well, she wished that and to not be in the company of men who'd openly planned her hanging.

"Now, according to your testimony," the priest said, gasping as he did so, "You were out here with the family and then the sky turned purple. What do you mean by that? Couldn't you have just said it was the evening?"

"No. I meant the air was purple. It was already dark out. It was like someone had turned on a second violet sun."

"Ah, so if that's the case, you mean you and the entire family were out here in the middle of the night. Why is that?"

"It's hard to explain in ways you'd understand."

"Because it's a blatant lie!" the assistant screamed.

The priest shushed him. "Enough of that. The truth we'll out. We'll give her enough rope…"

"And then I'll hang her myself."

The woods were harder to traverse than Eleanor remembered. She only remembered fleeing out of them. The five of them had run out of things to talk about, and the only words any of them muttered were cuss words and out-of-breath blasphemy as they pushed through nettles and brambles. In time, they made it to the clearing where it had happened, where Eleanor had abandoned a family in need.

She looked at the singed ground. The journalist walked from tree to tree and felt the bark. Sap had oozed out through the cracks in the wood. A scrape filled the silence as the assistant scraped his shoes against the rocks. The ground was singed. Eleanor lifted her head up to see the clearing was a near-perfect circle. The branches up above had melted away, leaving only smooth, black stubs.

"I must admit," the priest began. He caught his breath. There is something mighty peculiar about this spot. I hope you've all noticed we're standing in a ring."

"The ground's dead, too," the journalist offered. He tried to wipe the amber jelly from his fingers. "And so are these trees. It's like they got cooked from the inside out."

"I'm sure there's a reasonable explanation to all this," said the assistant. "Besides which, we're not here for horticulture. We led a whore to—"

"Can you just shut up for a minute?" said the journalist. "God, you're obsessed."

"Or what?"

Eleanor grasped the priest's hand. "This is where I saw them last. And the demons too. They were alive when I fled. Maybe they're still out here."

"Now if they was alive, how come they didn't run with you?"

"They were sick and had trouble breathing. Even if they tried, they wouldn't have been able to keep up. I must have waited for them outside the ranch for hours, but they never came. It's when the screaming started that I decided to hide inside. And that's how you found me."

The deputy nodded and turned to leave, turning around once more to speak. "This is what they call a fool's errand, men. I could have told you this was a waste of time before breakfast and saved us all a trip."

He walked back toward the ranch. The priest and the assistant followed. Eleanor spun around, trying to find something she had forgotten. She looked off into the woods and then down at her handcuffs.

"They don't care if you run," said the journalist.

"Of course not. How does it feel to be a part of a lynch mob?"

"It's not the best feelings, I'll say that much. It's surprising though. I mean, if they want you dead so badly, why have you spent so long in that cell?"

"The bodies. These people have a strange sense of decorum with corpses. Not a one of the cared none about these ranchers while they were alive. But the minute someone's dead, you've got a whole new outlook. That and they can't prove anything. Even a small town like that needs proof. 'Course, if I killed anyone, they'd have never suspected me."

"What's that now?"

"Just hypothetical is all. But if, and I mean if, I was going to kill someone, I'd be sure to make it look like an accident. People have accidents all the time. Someone catches dysentery or gets bitten by a snake or drowns, nobody suspects foul play."

"You, uh, do you think about people dying a lot?"

"Oh, no more than most, probably. Those three knucklefucks up yonder, though, now they have as serious a predilection for murder as ever I saw. Not you, though. I can tell you're different."

"Why thank you. And not that it alters the course of law, but in my book at least I consider you an innocent woman."

"Now let's not got that far. Not one of us is innocent as far as the eyes above are concerned."

"I suppose that's true, too."

They walked at a slower pace than those ahead, like lovers at the park. When they reached the ranch they were welcomed by a cacophony of expletives. Something had happened. The deputy and the assistant were shoving each other. Only the priest was trying to break them up. Eleanor and the journalist picked up pace and realised what was happening. The stagecoach was missing its horses and porters.

"That's enough, fellers, please," the priest was saying. They stopped their shoving match, more out of pity for the old man, who hunched forward and grasped his chest to steady his breathing.

"At least there's one thing you can't blame me for," Eleanor said.

They ignored her and all at once became children playing, tracking, ears pressed to the ground as they searched for hoofprints. Eleanor retreated to the side of the ranch and slid down the wall, watching their investigations unfold. She hadn't had so much fun watching men not know what to do since her eighteenth birthday. It was difficult to hide her amusement as they tried to call for the horses; the men tried to scry the events with the help of the sky. The only thing they hadn't seemed to notice was it had started to rain. She stood up and opened the ranch's door.

"It's raining, detectives," she told them.

Inside was stuffy and dank. The windows had been boarded shut since the family left. Everything of value had been taken, either by police or self-proclaimed grieving relatives. All that remained was the heaviest of the furniture and a handful of books. Eleanor sat down by the fire and wondered if they would let her burn something. She could hear them all outside. The journalist was getting the worst of it, starting sentences only to be talked over by one or all three of the others.

The journalist entered the house and for the second or so before he noticed Eleanor he seemed like a different person. He said nothing, instead preferring to run his fingers over the dust and the fading memories of the family who'd once called the place home.

The door flung open, and the deputy entered. "I am going to see if I can find the horses. Weather might benefit us just this once. I'll be taking the mayor's little friend with me, Eleanor, so you don't have to worry about an impromptu lynching just yet. We'll be back. Might as well try to get comfortable."

Eleanor held her hands up to him and jangled her chains.

The deputy stroked his upper lip with his thumb. He crouched beside her and unlocked her cuffs, tossing them and the key at the journalist who promptly dropped both. "Don't imagine even you would try running in these conditions. Take care." His voice was as close to friendly as it ever had been. He stood, spun, and left the house just as the priest was entering.

The three of them fast became familiar with the homestead. Scrawling nonstop on his notepad, the journalist went from room to room making notes and sketches, wondering with semi-audible sadness what the place must have been like with life inside it. He would stop at the spaces where heirlooms had sat and sigh to himself.

Meanwhile, the priest was struggling to build a fire. It was clear based on how he held lit matches over the lumber that he had lit nothing besides candles.

In the kitchen, Eleanor found a cupboard full of salted provisions and did her best to salvage a meal. She did this quietly. It was strange, given the circumstances, but she wanted to surprise the men with some food. This was not how she imagined the day going when she concocted her plan the night before. In some ways it was going better than expected. The porters stealing the horses had been a surprise boon.

After much struggling, the priest put a match into the kindling beneath the fire. He tried to hide how happy he was. The slither of a grin, the tilt in his eyes, the little jig he made while he walked to the chair, these were all things he tried to suppress. Warming his toes by the growing orange flame, his attention turned to his stomach. His voice rattled the rafters. "Say, is that food I smell?"

"I told you I was cooking," said Eleanor.

"Oh. You're cooking? I thought it was the nurse. Is she in there with you?"

"No."

The journalist poked his head into the room. "I bet she's still in the outhouse."

"Still? It's been hours. Someone better check on her." The priest paused, expecting someone to offer.

Eleanor entered with two warm mugs. Steam wafted from the rims. She'd been very lucky in the pantry. "Warm you up before you go? The storm's going to break any minute now. Can't you hear it?"

They could. The roof was sighing as the wind beat down on it. Raindrops the size of frogs were landing with the rat-tat of a regimental drummer.

"Thank ye," said the priest, swallowing the boiling liquid without a second thought. "You know, Eleanor, the more I see of you, the more I see of this place, the harder it is for me to believe in your guilt. I will share this with the others when they return with the horses."

"If they return, that is," said Eleanor. "No telling what trouble they've got themselves into out there. A right brain trust those two."

"Ah. Maybe I spoke too soon. Didn't have you pegged as a pessimist."

"I'm not. But thoughts turn bleak when you've been imprisoned for a crime for which you're totally innocent, you know."

The priest coughed. "There's some truth there. I will return."

He put his hands against the fire for a last time and then went outside. The downpour was unrelenting, and it was like watching a man render himself to the ocean as he stepped outside. Within three paces, he disappeared into the weather. The door wouldn't close, propped open by the wind. The journalist rushed to close it; his front consumed by the water while he did so. He could not see the old man outside.

"And then there were two," he said with a sheepish smile.

Eleanor tried to hand him the other mug. He took it only to set it on a barren windowsill. He returned to wandering the home like a wayward ghost, murmuring trite prose to himself all the while. It was like being haunted by a failed poet. Eleanor draped herself across the floor next to the fire. She hadn't felt genuine warmth in a long time.

Out loud, she wondered to herself, "You don't think whatever got that poor family is making the rounds snatching everyone outside, do you? Those other incidents you talked about, did any of them happen in the same place twice?"

The journalist stopped dead. "I'm going to be honest with you, I have no idea. This is my first reporting job and by the time I picked up the trail last month, most of the leads were long gone. Just a lot of hearsay and rumours. I guess I should be glad they held you for so long."

"Yeah, it's been grand."

"But to answer your question, no. I think the others can take care of themselves."

A pained scream broke through the outside torrent. It didn't stop. The scream continued in sharp jags, growing louder and louder until it burst through the door. Standing in the doorway was the drenched priest. He pointed and stammered toward a hidden horror. "It's the old lady. She's dead. Dead as a door mouse. Out in the outhouse."

The journalist threw his notepad to the floor and chased the priest outside. Eleanor lay there confused. She rolled over and crawled to the journalist's notes. She's a Witch, it said. Over and over. The word "witch" had been circled, as had other words such as "killer" and "succubus." Eleanor thumber through the other pages, hoping naively the words were about someone else.

All she found inside was sophomoric drivel. She grabbed a shawl from beside the fire and ran for the door at the rear of the house and sprinted off into the woods.

The old medicine woman's skirt was hitched up above her waist as she sat slumped on the outhouse bench, the bib of her blouse covered in wet, blood-flecked vomit, eyes purple and wide open, a red trail oozing out of each nostril. Her skin was bloated and red. She was dead, alright.

Father Pierce stood as close as he could, but the smell and the exposed shame both were too much for him to stomach. He darted behind the outhouse and vomited. The journalist could only stand there looking at the body, waiting for the preacher to finish his retching.

"Not much we can do out here until morning, father."

"Please, urgh, call me, blurgh…"

"We shouldn't leave that woman alone too long. She's the conniving type. No telling what she's up to."

The priest reappeared, pausing to wipe his mouth. "She was with one or both of us this whole time. There's a killer among us, to be sure, but it's not her."

The journalist pointed at the dead woman. "Someone poisoned her. I imagine if they hadn't buried those prisoners when they died, we'd have found out they were poisoned too. You don't need to be around to do something like that. Not unless you enjoy it."

"No idea a man of words would be so familiar with poisoning."

They entered the house. Their clothes were ruined and clung to their cold skin. The unattended fire was close to death. The priest was crestfallen. More importantly, Eleanor was gone. They scoured the home for some time but had to admit the truth to themselves.

"Still have your doubts, father?"

"I've seen innocent men run from far less. Maybe the mayor's friend came back and snatched her."

"Either way, we better find her."

They once more braved the rain. It was an unrelenting downward force, pushing them as best it could into the ground. They were too wet to notice. Trundling through the flooded mud and thick grass, they moved for the woods.

Protected by a heavy canopy above them, their walk in the woods was more manageable. The leaves caught much of the rain, sent down to the ground in streams. A single owl was calling out to them. It was harder to push through the thickets in the darkness.

They pushed forward to the opening and stood at the perimeter. The rain poured into the empty circle. A stream of water rolled by their feet as they stood there.

"There," the journalist pointed. Even as the rain obliterated the ground beneath them, the trail was unmistakable. Two feet had dug deep grooves into the earth. The bushes at the far side of the circle had been torn apart in a hurry. "We can't be far behind her."

The priest hadn't recovered since vomiting and was just about doubled over as he stood beside the journalist. One hand gripped his bent knee, the other propped him up by leaning against the journalist. He couldn't catch his breath. His lungs rattled with every exhalation. "Ill wait here in case she turns around," he said. Then he tumbled forward and lay on the ground. He lay there refusing to stand up, his chest was moving with increasing irregularity.

"Are you good?"

"She won't spot me if I'm lying down. Trust me." Water pooled around his side as he lay there. He tried to blink away the rain. "Just find her and make sure she's safe."

"You have my word, father."

"Please call me…"

But the journalist was already following what he thought was a trail.

The deputy returned alone to the homestead. They had found the two porters and horses not too far from the ranch. All dead. The bodies lay slumped on the side of the road with no signs of trauma. Then the rain worsened, and the assistant muttered something about needing to rush off ahead, doing exactly that before the deputy could stop him. The deputy had the immense pleasure of walking back in the rain with only his gone and his darkening thoughts for company.

By the time he'd reached the homestead, he was happy he'd solved the case. Little good it would to him. The Eleanor woman, he'd surmised, was a vagrant, and both she and the missing family were victims of a malicious scheme. Someone wanted the land. There'd been rumours of wild outlaws living in the woods. Perhaps they'd been paid to murder and burn the family. It would account for the fiery circle in the woods.

Yes, that was it. The family had caught the woman foraging for food in the woods, and the ensuing argument had attracted a group of mountain men who promptly drugged the poor woman and butchered the landowners. The porters had probably been drugged too.

He hoped the assistant was involved so he could shoot him.

All these theories made it with him to the homestead and lasted right until he found the medicine woman dead in the shitter. She'd been poisoned too. And burnt. Her skin was dissolving into her pink flesh.

He knew he was in the thick of it, and he knew there was no way out.

First, he rushed through the house, hoping to either find the others or their bodies. Then he followed the wet prints on the ground. He stopped at the door, found himself a lantern, checked his gun, and walked down the trail.

The journalist was lost in the woods. He knew the trail had gone cold, or he did not understand what he was doing. One of the two. He was left stumbling in the cold, wetness darkness of the ancient woods. Alone except for the sounds of his breath and that one owl far about. A rumble of distant thunder. The sky lit up. His surroundings were illuminated but offered no help. One soaking branch looks much like another.

He considered collapsing and watching the sky above as the storm grew worse. Perhaps he could force himself to sleep and try again in the morning. This, he knew, was his own mind trying to betray him. His mind had been betraying him for a few hours, by his estimate. Hours? Maybe. He.

He couldn't remember what he was doing. His skin was hot. Why was he vomiting?

The deputy had no difficulty walking through the woods. With the confident strides of a trained warrior, he found the clearing just in time to hear the priest sputter up blood. He rushed to the holy man's side, but it was already too late. The priest was dying. His skin was blistered and pustulating. He tried to grab at the deputy, to say some parting words, but all that came out were the weak puh-puh-puhs of a man who'd already died.

"The hell is going on," the deputy said to himself.

Eleanor sat under a rock and tried to plan her next move. She had no idea what to do, propelled as she was by instinct. If they weren't already looking for her, they would be. Even in a torrential storm. She had no options. Only woods and mountains and a town that thought she was a murderer. She couldn't go back there, obviously. Her own poor impulses had cemented her guilt.

Someone coughed nearby.

She crawled out from under the rock and looked around. It was the journalist. He was staggering, stumbling toward nothing, whispering to himself all the while. Lightning filled the sky and revealed him. His face had become blotchy and red. From a distance, it looked like his hair was falling out.

"Hey," she called out.

The journalist turned to face her. Yes, his hair was sliding down his face and the rain poured down. He didn't seem to notice. His eyes almost broke Eleanor's heart. They looked like the eyes of a wounded puppy. Confused and dying.

"It's OK," she said. "I can help you, I'm sure. Take my hand."

She held out her hand, and after a few missed swipes, he grasped it. His flesh was bulbous, slimy even. Eleanor tried to act as if it didn't bother her.

It occurred to her that lightning dissipates. Tends to. The last strike still lingered in the air, revealing the woods in their entirety. The light, she noticed, was purple. It did not go away.

The deputy fell to his knees as the beam of light scorched his skin. He tried to cover his flesh, but he could tell he was baking from the inside. His head was swimming with flashing memories and blurred phantoms. He couldn't tell where hallucinations ended and the otherworldly calamity surrounding him began. He lay there twitching, gasping for air, and saw Eleanor step into the centre of the clearing. What remained of the journalist tried to follow her.

If his mental capacity was less diminished, he may have noticed it was no longer raining above him. Something was blocking the weather. Something above the searing light. Eleanor looked over at him.

"Sorry," she said. "Thought you'd be gone for a while."

The light flashed, blinding the deputy. When he opened his eyes, the light vanished. The rain fell again. Eleanor and the journalist were gone.

He could feel his lungs melt. The icy waters from the sky were hissing against his baked skin. With what strength he had left, he rolled over to his back and looked up at the sky. The lightning was coming in fast. Amidst the flashing lights, he could see a spherical thing floating off into the heavens. He smiled. Maybe he wasn't cut out for detective work. He put the barrel of his gun in his mouth and—

It was sunrise before the assistant to the mayor returned to the ranch. Rain and crevices had waylaid him, having fallen down a small hill after running from the deputy. What a miserable night. Reaching the building, he hoped to see a set of relieved faces waiting for him. It was not to be so. He didn't notice the medicine woman as he entered the house. When he discovered it was empty, he followed the footprints into the woods.

The storm had damaged the land far less than he expected. Very few branches had fallen, even fewer trees. The ground was like molasses. A bunch of puddles and ponds had grown, but not too bad. Not too bad at all.

There was nothing good waiting for him out there. Nor would there be anything good waiting for him upon his return to town. What with him being the only survivor of a massacre and all.

Upon a Midnight

"That was just about the dumbest shit I've ever heard. Flying lights? Grey men? What have you been smoking? And do you have any more?"
"Ha. It really happened. You can ask about it at the town any time you want. They'll vouch for me."
"Vouch for a story where everyone died? Sure, pal. Besides, we have to get out of this shithole before we can do anything. No offence, barkeep."
"Yeah, but hey, since we've got your attention, how about another round of drinks? And speaking of drinking, picture it—"

A saloon lit up with candles and an open fireplace. Walls decked in red velvet curtains, mahogany, and mounted trophies. Two floors. On the bottom, the bar and a floor filled with raucous revellers. Ale flowed freely, seeping over the rims of glasses, tables, and slack mouths all the same. No one paid any attention to the mess. Not only could it wait until the morning, but it was someone else's problem. Shoes hammered hard on the oaken floorboards like the cloven hooves of Satan himself spread out over a hundred progeny. New and old friends danced with the same gayness as the pianist, and his minstrels revisited the town's favourite jaunts. Secrets some thought would remain hidden to the grave were blurted out from one drunken mouth or another. Money flew like autumn leaves.

On the second floor, three empty rooms, a balcony, and a private area. From the wooden banister, mayor Fortenberry looked down on his constituents. In his mind, he was the guest of honour. Few down below even knew he was there. The mayor's two loyal favourites stood guard over the stairs to ensure none of the riffraff entered their self-imposed den. In due time, when minds were loose and morals just the same, mayor Fortenberry would select a dozen of the younger guests for a more sophisticated celebration.

The only person not celebrating sat on the ground level at a dark corner of the bar. A stranger, new to town. He tapped his feet to the rhythm of the music and surveyed the spectacle behind him through a cracked mirror. His own tired reflection was the one thing he could not bring himself to look at. Soon he would have to speak to a crowd who would come to hate him.

Fortenberry tossed a string of meaningless syllables over the balcony, and the musicians stopped their gaiety. The chuntering continued. Mayor Fortenberry called down for attention and received none in return. Not until his second man loosed two bullets into a stuffed deer's head. The rabble stopped their talking.

"Your attention please, my kind and noble citizens!"

The mayor smiled at his inferiors. They stared back slack jawed and half drunk, swaying almost with synchronicity as they waited on the mayor to get it over with. "Brothers and sisters of this most splendid of towns, thank you all so much for your patronage tonight!"

Vacant, dull eyes looked up at him. His smile faltered. None of them had come to listen to a rich man pontificate. Except, perhaps, for the stranger at the bar who tilted his head sideways to better hear.

"Now, as you folks no doubt know, this town of ours means a lot to me. My mother, Lord rest her soul, was the first true owner of the land we're standing on right now. My father, Lord rest his soul, was the first to till the soil outside. It is fitting their beloved son would become this wondrous town's first elected mayor. My brother—"

"Lord rest his soul!"

A few murmurs from the crowd. There had been rumours, but... The mayor's eyes darted, defensive and feral, and his men clasped the handles of their revolvers and made their way down the stairs. "Who SAID that?"

Neighbour eyeballed neighbour, but nobody came forward nor offered up their fellow man. It was the neighbour, after several baited moments, who pushed his stool away and sauntered into the middle of the room. He raised his hand. Those closest to him moved away from him until they could no longer move.

The mayor looked him over as his two favourites pushed through the masses. "I don't recall seeing your face around here before."

"That's because you ain't seen it before, you old crook."

"Then who gave you the right to waltz into MY town and sling these foul aspersions on my brother while these good people are trying to celebrate my hard-fought success? I'll have you know my sweet brother is alive and well in Connecticut right now on the most important business, and you sully my family's name by implying his death."

The stranger laughed. "It's always the guilty who talk the most. You ever notice?" He turned his back to the mayor and faced the town's citizens. "Friends, this man is a liar. Even as we speak, his sweet brother's eyes are being devoured by rats in that overstocked cellar of his. And for what reason? Greed. Mister Fortenberry is—"

"Enough, sir. We have humoured your drunken buffoonery for long enough, it's time for you to go."

Two sets of hands grasped the stranger and tried to usher him toward the exit.

Sweating, shaken, trying to remain calm, the mayor grasped the balcony with white knuckled tightness to mask his shaking palms. "I apologise for this irrelevant drunk, my friends. The next round is on me. Drink up you all. Gerald, the keys please, make it a merry song."

Gerald played the piano.

The stranger pushed himself free. "No. No!" he screamed. The flames grew, the rafters shook, even the ground outside trembled to the sound of the stranger's voice. Everything turned silent. "Irrelevant? Me? Mister, my good friend, if you died right here tonight you would be replaced by the morning and forgotten about by the end of the day on Thursday. And you know this. You know this. And you stand up there and presume to judge me? Me? You know nothing of who I am or what I am capable. No, sir. But I know you. I know exactly who you are Henry James Fortenberry. You are a liar, a fraud, a collector of young girls' innocence, a murderer, a—"

A shot rang out. The stranger clutched at his chest and fell to his knees. Gasping, he looked around the room for the source of the bullet. His eyes locked with the mayor's as the bastard blew the smoke from his golden pistole and traipsed down the stairs. The two favourites grasped the stranger's shoulders and held him in place.

"A bullet's not enough to kill you? Very well. All the better for me."

The partygoers stood enthralled as the mayor and his two men beat the wounded stranger, digging their heels into his soft tissue, his joints. The mayor slapped him, spat at him, finally stomping on his face as he lay motionless on the ground as if trying to eradicate all trace of the slanderer.

After several minutes, Fortenberry fell back to his knees, breathless and glistening. He looked first at his trembling hands and then at the onlookers. He blinked and turned his attention to the bar. "I sure am sorry you all had to see that. He left me no choice. You all saw! But to make it up to you, the drinks are on me for the rest of the night."

He walked to the bar; the partygoers pushing and pulling at each other, all barking their orders for fresh drinks. They had all but forgotten about what they had just witnessed. For a moment.

A woman shrieked and fainted. The crowd turned to see the stranger, untouched and indifferent, standing over the bodies of Fortenberry's men. In each hand, the stranger held the dripping red workings of the fallen men's throats. He dropped the tracheas onto their former owners and wiped the blood on his jacket before pointing at the mayor. "I will get to you in a minute, Henry, but first," he looked at the drunks, "You are all complicit now. I want you to watch what is about to happen. If one of you so much as looks at the exit, I will destroy you and all you claim to cherish. Are we clear?"

A few murmured. Some even helped shove the stammering, sorrowful mayor toward the stranger.

"You don't have to do this, you fuck," said Fortenberry.

"Oh, but I do," the stranger replied, resting his thumbs against the man's pulsing temples. "Now watch everyone. The first to turn away dies next."

And watch they did. In silence. They watched at all the pomp and bravado the mayor once possessed ebbed away as he shrunk and slumped to the floor. His last words were pitiful pleas and childish threats, but they soon gave way much as the very essence of his being gave away. The stranger was crushing him with his bare hands, savouring it too, in no rush to end the man's life. For twenty minutes, the stranger broke mayor Fortenberry and for twenty minutes to former revellers watched.

In time, the old mayor lay surrounded by his pooling blood and effluvia. The stranger stepped back and looked upon his witnesses. He gestured at the three corpses. "These men meant to kill me, good people, and not a one of you could muster the strength to raise a hand to help me. You could not help a brother in need? You all knew the truth about this so-called mayor long before I appeared. For shame. You should all be ashamed."

A few tried to apologise, but the stranger did not care. Instead, he walked to the musicians. "Sirs, your music was of the highest order tonight and I must insist that you and you alone wait for me just a little outside. I won't be long. Please take your instruments."

"Sir?" said Gerald.

"Oh, right, the piano? I'll get that. But run along now, we have a little time."

The musicians obliged. The other partygoers stood enraptured and still. The stranger walked to the fireplace and then turned to face them.

"As for the rest of you."

The musicians stood in the dirt of the town's main track as fire licked up the sides of the saloon. The only things to escape were the unrelenting heat of the flames and the screams of those inside. The door pushed open. A man appeared. The stranger. He was unmoved by the fires. As was the piano he was dragging behind him. He pulled it off the wood and onto the dirt road, dragging it until he reached Gerald.

"See? I told you it would only take a minute."

"Those poor people inside, sir."

"What about them?"

"You massacred them."

The stranger smiled and nodded like a buffoon. "Yes, I did."

"But I don't understand why."

The stranger waved off Gerald's concerns and guided the musicians to their instruments. He hummed a simple tune and waved at them until they followed along. The upbeat music felt almost like a dirge accompanied as it was by the desperate last screams coming from the saloon. The stranger danced around the band. "You see, my friends, there are two types of people in this world." He shook and gyrated as his feet drew rings around the band.

"Good and evil," offered Gerald.

"No such thing," the stranger said, fingers waving in the air above his head. "No. Those who have music in their souls. People like you and I." He spun around. The musicians all but forgot about the murders and found themselves engrossed in the dance.

"And the second type, sir?"

The stranger had become lost in his feverish dance. "Come on, now, we've talked enough for now. We're here to dance and nothing else!"

The pianist nodded, and they continued to play. Up tempo. Energetic. Joyful. The stranger's circle of dancing grew wider as he spun and shimmied around the fiery wreckage of the saloon. Unsupervised children, left along so their parents could drink, appeared as did the town's many uninvited. They joined the stranger in his dancing and he convulsed and gesticulated and moved in ways the band had never seen before. The surviving townspeople danced glorious loops around the inferno led by the stranger and the musicians' virtuoso performance.

The stranger broke away from the line of dancers and returned to Gerald. He patted him on the back. "The damned," he said. "Now you best play until daybreak and all will be well. You have my word."

He walked down the road. The fire behind his crackled and roared as it found fresh food to feast upon. The dancing survivors showed now signs of tiring, nor did the musicians and their plucky tunes.

With the procession and the upbeat accompaniment fading behind him, the stranger walked out of town. He looked through every door and window he crossed paths with. There would come a time when he would need to return to the town, and he needed to be sure all who remained knew of his deeds.

He walked in a straight line without concern for what he stepped on. Road, dirt, river, it was all the same to him. The sky was moonless. Starless. For many, such darkness was enough to draw out prayers for fire or daylight. He was not the praying kind. Had not been for some time. A man of both worlds, he inhabited the darkness just as he did the light. Call it attuned senses or something far more preternatural, but his vision was exemplary. He could see the crickets chirping in their thickets, the vapours of long departed horses, recognise every footstep, every track mark, every broken twig.

He reached the crossroads. As expected, young Billy sat on the remnants of a boulder wall and strummed his violin. A small fire sat on the ground nearby, inching ever closer to oblivion. A lantern hung from a branch, illuminating the ragged tent the boy had slept in. The crossroads had become a meeting point of sorts, and it was best to appear as impoverished as possible while you waited there. Few would care to notice a pauper sleeping in the tattered memory of a tent.

"Is that you, Mister Cross?" Billy called out, grey eyes staring off into the unknown.

The stranger was taken aback. He was trying to manoeuvre himself just so before revealing himself, his body engulfed as it was by shadows and his footsteps quieter than the cicada in the long grass. Billy was a sharp one, he had to give him that much.

"Yes, Billy. I am here. No need to be alarmed."

"I'm not alarmed, y'old goat."

"All the same."

Mister Cross, the stranger, stepped into the glow of the fire. He smiled at the boy, at his prized fiddle. Stepping over the flames, he straddled the wall beside the boy and folded his arms, letting out an expectant cough.

"Well, I just about failed in your request, sir, but I've done it. I wrote and performed the song you ast for."

"Indeed. I am thankful for your help. But that's not the only song you've been singing. Is it? Billy?"

"I don't know what the hell you're talking about."

"Oh, come on, boy, I'm not one of those village idiots you hoodwink. Did you think a man of my capabilities wouldn't find out what lies you've been spreading?"

Billy held his fiddle close and shuddered. He faced the fire, as if that would extinguish Mister Cross' existence. "No, no, sir. I did as you ast. I sang of your deeds in every town I walked through. I told them all about you. It's what you requested, and I did nothing more besides."

Mister Cross spat into the fire. "You've been telling those bumpkins you won that fiddle in a battle of wits against me. Haven't you?"

"I mean, but mister, sir, you didn't say nothing contrary to such saying so as much did you, I don't reckon."

"Your jumbled words might work for some, Billy, but you should know better than to try them on me. We had an arrangement, boy, written in blood. You were to sow the seeds of my name into the hearts of men so they might expect my return. And what? You've painted me as a rambling jester. A fool. A devil. How are they to relish my arrival if they believe a blind urchin can best me?"

"I did as you ast."

"No, lad."

"But, I, you, I—"

The boy's words trailed off as Mister Cross stood upright. The man's eyes had become a dark amber. Two incinerators where pupils should be. "Have you any comprehension of the harm you've caused? Did you think you could trick and plot against something of my power? You impudent—"

"Now, sir, it got people talking. That's what you wanted!"

"And now in your last moments you deign to interrupt me? Get on your feet, Billy."

"I don't wanna."

"Billy."

The boy dug his ankles into the gaps between the rocks and wrapped his wrists against his precious violin. "Now, sir, listen, there ain't no call for this."

Mister Cross laughed. "There's no reason for anything, boy. The universe is a frantic dance and chaos is the band. But we had a contract, you and I, and you saw fit to not only sully my name but to go against your word. Your word, Billy. The only thing worth anything in this universe is the word. Your word. And you threw it away like yesterday's paper."

"Paper?"

"Silence. Stand up."

"Now hold on, I can think of a way to make this right by you."

"You're testing my patience." Mister Cross stepped into the dwindling fire. The flames burst into life, illuminating the crossroads with a bright orange. "Now."

"Aw, hell, Mister Cross, you don't think people are going to respond to you more fondly if they know you've got a sense of humour?"

"Oh, I've been humouring you for long enough, lad. But that is irrelevant. This is the last chance to stand up, Billy. There are far worse fates than what is waiting for you."

Billy's mind raced for one final excuse, a phrase or suggestion that might save his life, but there was nothing left to say. Defeated, he slid off his perch and landed on his feet. He stood there wobbling. "Does it help if I say I am sorry?"

Mister Cross stroked his thumbs with his index fingers. "Yes, it does, Billy. But you called me the devil, Billy. The devil. If not for that, your soul may well have survived. I have not endured—and Lord knows I've endured—what I have only for you to besmirch me in such a way. I gave you the violin as a kindness, yes? No trick, correct? I didn't threaten or cajole you, did I? No. I sought you out because your music is divine. And yet here we are."

Billy dropped the violin at Cross' feet. "You can have it back if that's all you're after. I didn't mean nothing by it."

"No, but one never does. Actions have consequences, though, Billy. Intended or otherwise. That's my word. And I would be a hypocrite if I went against it. I hope you understand."

"I just thought we were friends is all."

"Then you shouldn't have lied to me. Will you stop trying to weasel your way out of this and take your punishment as a man?"

Billy pulled a revolved from the back of his pants and pointed it, in shaking fashion, at the honourable Mister Cross. "You don't come one step closer, you hear?"

"Billy. Billy." Mister Cross stepped over the fire and reached out for Billy. The boy fired twice. Unflinching, Cross continued to walk until his body all but consumed the boy. "It's funny how many of you, in these last moments, mistake braggadocio for bravery. It never works. You could have died a good man, Billy, but now you die a coward. Goodnight, old friend."

"Fuck you," said Billy, firing until the chambers were spent.

Mister Cross' judgement was fast. Billy's eyes spasmed and bulged and leaked bitter tears and blood and membranous pulp, his face contorted into the embodiment of pain, his screams lost themselves in the caverns of his thorax, his organs throbbed and shuddered and oozed blood and bile. The mischievous synapses in the boy's brain fired off like a lightning storm and all at once his cherished memories vanished, fried, obliterated, his dying mind retreating ever further into the recesses of his subconscious so that every second became an eternal fever dream. Inside, Billy's laughing family, his friends, the sounds of his favourite songs, the touch of a woman all evaporated. Outside, the body that had been Billy convulsed and shat upon the ground. Billy, blasphemer, liar, musician, was dead long before his final breath whistled out the bulbous remnants of his lungs. His fingers danced as a pianist's would across the crabgrass, his feet jigging over the edges of the fire. One last dance.

Mister Cross placed the violin on the boy's chest and then walked to the next town in search for another fool.

Flop

Milton slammed his cards on the table. It hadn't been going his way. Half of his money was about to go elsewhere. "Aw horseshit!"

"What? Brat like that got what he deserved as far as I'm concerned."

"Naw, this hand's what's horseshit. I can't pull a suited anything for the life of me. But… yeah, I guess I could do with less of these Mister Cross stories. He's a walking freakshow."

"Yeah," added John. "Him and that Lawman idiot both. I want more women fighting monsters and shit like that."

"Ah, I'm sorry," said Alfredo, "They've been on my mind is all."

"How come?" John leaned in. "That Cross gentleman frame you for murder? The Lawman coming to get you?"

"What? Coming to get me? No. Nothing like that."

"Then, wh—"

Joshua stood up, the liquor in control of everything south of his liver. "You know, it wouldn't surprise me to learn one of them was on their way here, the way today has played out." He walked to the doors. "Now, if you'll all excuse me a moment, I need to go water the flowers."

He pushed the doors open and stepped outside. The sun tore into the building, as bright as it had been. The other three shielded their eyes as the doors swung closed and listened to the salesman groan as he struggled to find a dark corner.

"You got flowers out there?" Milton asked the bartender.

The bartender shrugged.

"Anyway," Milton continued. "You ask me, and this is assuming they're actual people, but in my mind I reckon Cross and this Lawman are the same person. Someone with a warped sense of justice roving the land and murdering the common folk. I bet he ays people to tell them these stories. Makes out he's some righteous demon when I bet he's a little pissant like old Josh out there."

John dealt another hand. He tossed the cards like a rookie dealer, as if focused on something else. Gone was his riverboat special, his deck defying flourish.

"Speaking of, shouldn't we wait on him?" Alfredo asked, looking over at the door.

"Nah. He can miss the one hand. This game's about over anyway," John said, adding, "This one's just for the three of us desperados. Just the three of us. Best leave him out there pissing on his boots. Let's make it interesting, though. Five cards each, no draw, no ante? What do you say?"

The three men looked at their hands. Alfredo nodded at his cards and tossed in a small bet. Milton matched. John raised. Alfredo raised again.

"Waste of damned time," said Milton, throwing his cards down again.

"All in," said John. "So anyway, Al, how long you been searching for Cross? Months? Years? What made you think you'd find him out here?"

Alfredo looked at his cards, at Milton, at the bartender, at the wall being hit by a steady stream of urine. Everywhere but John's accusatory glare. "I don't comprende," he said, folding.

"A bit late for the act, bud," John said. He raked in his winnings and then flipped over Alfredo's dead hand. "That right there's a straight flush, Al. In the business we call that a winning hand."

"So? You won."

"So I've had you pegged since we all sat down here this… when? Hey, barkeep, when did we all show up here?"

"Morning before last, I reckon," the bartender said.

"That doesn't seem right," John said, trailing off for a moment before capturing the words he'd carefully concocted. "I know your type, Al, is what I am saying. You're not the bluffer you think you are, and you ain't no damn fugitive neither."

"OK. I'm a bum. You have to learn how to snarl when there are danger-ous dogs around," Alfredo's hands disappeared under the table.

"You're no bum. You can try to look as rough as you want, but your hands have told a different story this whole damn time. Look at 'em. Show Milton your hands."

Alfredo's eyes met John's for the first time in hours. He remained motion-less until John flashed the polish of his own revolver. "Just humour me, Alfredo. Do you mind, Milton?"

"You two have been flirting all day. Leave me out of this."

"You're going to look at this sonofabitch's hands, Milton. And you're going to show him."

"Fine, John, whatever you say." Alfredo removed his hands from under the table and showed his palms to Milton. They were fair and unblemished. Not a callus or scar in sight. They were the hands of an office clerk, the nou-veau riche, the sanctimonious.

Milton looked at the hands and clucked. "So the man's got baby hands. What of it?"

John stood up; his revolver still aimed in the vague direction of Alfredo. "Think rationally, Milton. We don't even know how long we've been here. We keep sharing stories of wandering sheriffs and vigilante preachers. It's a setup. We've been set up. Something foul is at play in this town, my man. And I reckon it's all down to this liar right here."

The bartender came around the corner of his bar with his shotgun ready. "Now, lads, I've warned you once about—" he never finished the sentence. A bullet bore a hole through his face, shattering the shelf of whiskeys behind him. He stood there for a moment, the cavernous hole in his head spilling flu-ids down the front and back of his shirt, half his brain sliding down the newly shattered mirror behind the bar. And then he fell.

"Jesus, kid, what the hell are you doing?" Milton was standing now. Alfredo, too. Their hands had found their own weapons, and they both pointed at John.

Joshua ran back into the room and turned white in an instant. He instinc-tively leaned against the nearest wall and slid down it, murmuring to himself.

John kept his gun on Alfredo. He glanced at Joshua. "Stay right there, bud, I'm about to save your life. Someone's played us all."

"You've been out here too long," said Alfredo.

"You've lost your damned mind," Milton agreed.

"No. This is the clearest things have been in a while. We're all sinners here. Tricked into coming to this fake town where there'd be no witnesses. One of us isn't who they said they were. And that's you, Alfredo."

Alfredo looked around, inching backwards to the wall. "We're all liars here."

"But only three of us sinners. These stories we've been sharing, I figure they all have some truth to them. Joshua down there, he's a salesman, yes? But selling what? I'd wager slaves perhaps, or maybe he was the one what sold those settlers that phony map. Milton. Well, his story about the dead boy. Angus, weren't it? He got a little too emotional about that one. I figure him for poor Angus' brother."

Milton lowered his weapon. "It's true."

"Oh, yeah, and who does that make you?" Alfredo said.

With his free hand, John unbuttoned his shirt and opened it wide, exposing a series of vicious scars. Chunks of his flesh were missing. The right side of his torso was a silken peach field of dead tissue. "We didn't quite get to my story, but take it from me when I say I'm not a good person. That just leaves you, Alfredo."

"That doesn't mean I've tricked us all into coming here. How'd I even do that if it were possible?"

John shrugged. "Tell me I'm wrong."

Alfredo was frozen in time, scanning his options and whispering prayers to himself. "You're caught up in something you don't understand, John. It's not too late to calm down. Nobody will miss the body there, but people will miss me. And they'll come for you."

"Come for me? And how are they to do that?"

"Please, just get a grip of yourself before it's too late. I'm the only thing stopping you from damnation."

John sneered. "Maybe I want the damnation." He unloaded his bullets into Alfredo's chest. The poor man flailed silently as he toppled backwards and slammed into the wooden wall. He slid down to the ground, leaving a fetching red painting behind as he did so.

Milton lumbered over to the fallen man and searched his pockets. He found something and held it in the air. John squinted at the metallic trinket, seeing after a while it was a badge of sorts.

"You've just murdered a government man, you fool," Milton growled. "I ought to shoot you myself."

Something about these words uncorked the depths of John's psyche. He dropped his weapon and fell to his knees. Tears welled up in his eyes, held there through sheer masculine bravado. He looked imploringly at the giant. "Please," he said. "Please," he begged.

Joshua murmured from the confines of his foetal position, "John, I will be the one to kill you."

"The hell you will," said Milton. He stepped over to John and hoisted him up to his feet. "Is that what this is all about? A cry for help? Two dead men because you want to die? It'd be easier to just shoot yourself. Fairer for all involved too."

"No. I can't die by my hand. I've tried. Believe me."

Milton looked down at John, at the two corpses, at the trembling Joshua. "All right. But we're going to do this the old-fashioned way. You and me. Outside. Ten paces. And then I'll set you free, boy."

John nodded and picked up his gun, reloading it as he walked outside. Milton followed him, stopping at the doorway to look over at Joshua. "If you can handle it, would you oblige me in adjudicating this duel? Once that's cleared up maybe you can explain to me what your game is."

Joshua smiled. He rose to his feet and accompanied the giant outside. "Oh, you're good, Milton. A little too good. You best be careful around John. He's not what he thinks he is."

"I'm sure I'll be fine."

Shoes to Fill

"You're hiding your true nature," Randall said as he hitched up his pants and walked over to the window. Outside was full of life. It was a market day and vendors had come from all over the parish to sell their wares.

"They'd hang us." Milton was still in the bed, his furry chest damp with sweat. His beard covered most of his face, but the red welts from the night before could be seen darkening.

Randall turned. His eyes glowed with the tears of recognition. "I'm not talking about that, love. City life."

"What of it?"

"It's not for you. We both know it. That's why you go out fighting."

"These city men can't handle me."

"Oh, that's only true of most of them. I can handle you just fine." They smiled. "When did you last visit your family?"

Milton sat upright. "Aw hell, a decade plus. Can't stand the sight of dad as much as anything."

Randall sat on the bed beside him. "Does he still blame you?"

"For Angus? I'm sure he does. But it's not that. You ever see a cicada's shell? After it's broken out and moved on? That's my dad. Or at least it was. Don't imagine he got much better. Mom was never the same neither. It's like a part of her died when Angus did."

"And what about you?"

"What about me?"

"You ever take a moment for yourself to mourn? It has hurt to lose him so young."

"I mourn him every day in my own way."

"Well, that's good, love. I'm glad."

They looked at the door on the far side of the room. Randall stood and dressed. He still put his clothes on like a child and between that and his size he was hard to miss. It suited them. A giant hairy man and a dandy fop. No one would think to put them together.

"Milton. The fighting…"

"Don't start, Randy. It's a beautiful day outside. Was thinking we could buy you a new vase. Maybe walk along the river. I know a good fishing spot."

Randall swallowed his words. "That sounds wonderful. But Milton…"

"Yeah?"

"Please think about visiting your family. I'm sure your sisters miss you."

Milton strode over to the supine Randall and grasped his face with both his massive hands. He kissed him. "I'll think about it."

"Good."

"Oh, and Randy?"

"Yeah?"

"Thank you."

The rest of the day was good until it wasn't. They walked into the plaza just as the market stalls opened and already the grounds were packed with people. It was hard for them to ignore the stares of inquisitive strangers. Randall peacocked and exuberant, bedecked in white silks, his diamond-studded cane in one hand, his fine leather gloves in the other, face powdered and fragranced and puckered. Milton, the giant, taller even than some stalls, walking side by side with a sugarplum fairy, his face bruised, body a monument to the platonic ideal of mountain men.

They stopped first at the food stalls. Seventeen countries were represented, and the aromatic fog of spices were enough to satiate the hungriest of men. People would stop them, offering free samples and smiles.

"Try this," said one vendor after another. They did. Some were good, some divine, some terrible, although they disagreed which was which. Milton had never grown a fondness for spices, while Randall would engorge himself on the hottest foods he could find. He had plans to use his family fortune to set up a restaurant that would fuse the greatest foods on earth together. Curried jambalaya. Jerked chicken knishes. Peking goat.

"All I want is a steak and some potatoes," Milton said.

Randall laughed. "At a market? Besides, steak? We both know you eat cows whole."

"That was one time."

"Hush."

Their hands hovered ever closer to each other as they walked deep into the smoke-filled section of the stalls. People were selling candles and incense sticks, bound bunches of foxglove and clover. A small caravan hid between stalls and an old woman was reading palms. Another old woman had set up a table beside a statue and was reading cards.

Randall looked pleadingly at Milton.

Milton stroked the whiskers away from his mouth. "Fine."

They sat and handed the old woman her coins. She had them both draw a card. Milton selected the ten of swords. Randall chose the five of pentacles. The old woman looked at the cards and for a while said nothing.

"Well?"

"Oh!" she said. "These mean your new line of work will thrill you."

"All right."

Milton walked away.

The market was growing too loud for Milton to stand. Randall reached up to pat his shoulder and winked. They walked through the masses heading south to the river. There they stood, watching the sun's reflection ripple on the water. A few older men were fishing for their supper. Randall caught Milton staring at the men.

"You had this look when we were by the furs, too, you know."

"What look?"

"I don't know. Wistful. Like you'd rather be out there hunting."

"Uh-huh."

"I meant what I said earlier. You know I'm right. Deep down inside, you're starting to feel trapped. It's why you're banned from every watering hole in town. It's why the head of police knows you by name."

"But you're here."

Randall blushed beneath his lacquered face. "Still. Maybe I can move out somewhere with you. Sell some businesses. We'll get a ranch up in the plains."

"Raise sheep?"

"Raise horses."

"Now you're talking."

"And we'll have ourselves a stream that goes all the way out to a massive lake. We'll row down it one weekends. And the woods—"

"No woods."

"Fine. Fine. But what do you say? We can be ourselves out there. There'd be nobody around to judge us."

"It sounds like a slice of heaven. But it would kill you? Wouldn't it? Not being the society man, I mean."

Randall looked out at the water. "I'm getting old, love. I'm starting to look like a clown. There's no harm in me switching to denims. I bet you'd even like me dressed like that."

Milton grinned. "Just overalls and nothing else?"

"For you, anything."

Perhaps the two men had become too familiar with each other in that moment. Perhaps an idle touch had caught someone's attention. Or perhaps even the sight of a giant and a man dressed as a French aristocrat was too much to stomach for a group of young men. At any rate, five men had caught wind that they were there by the lake and announced themselves quickly.

"Hey, what's up with this freakshow," said one boy.

"I didn't think they could sell fruit this far from market," said another.

"Yeah, they, uh, they, um, the harbour is down that way," a third.

Milton pivoted and clenched his fists, only stopped by Randall's cane. "Gentlemen, wonderful weather today, yes?" Randall asked the boys. "Shame to ruin the moment."

"Listen, lady," the apparent ringleader said, "We're talking to the savage here."

Randall laughed until he didn't. Milton pushed his cane away and approached the men. "This isn't a fight you want," he said to them.

"Oh yeah? There's five of us and only one of you."

"One and a half," another boy corrected.

The fight was short-lived. Each boy succumbed to a single blow. They lay in a pile, groaning at Milton's feet. He inhaled sharply, catching his breath, fists clenched, still wanting to fight. He realised too late Randall had never seen him fight before. Until that moment it had been a fabled fact, something not quite real. His love stood there dumbfounded. A policeman not too far away was blowing a whistle. One boy was not moving.

Randall grasped Milton's arms and looked into his eyes. "You didn't need to do that."

"I know."

"And now everything is ruined."

"I know."

"You have to get out of the city."

"I… I know."

"But I'll be here waiting for you. I promise. Go visit your family. Clear your head. Quell the demons. I'll take care of things here."

"Right."

Milton stepped back and ran. He stopped.

"Oh, and Milton?"

"Yeah?"

"I love you."

Milton's smile broke through his thick beard. "You too." And off he ran, Randall using all his pomp and swagger to stop the approaching officers. One boy screaming about his neck, about his wealthy father, about his limp friend. All was chaos. Milton hoped he was running toward somewhere quieter.

For a time, his wish was granted. The road to New Bethlehem was long and often not a road. All was good. Milton walked straight and proud. During his walks, he would stop to take in the dung-less air, listen to the birds, enjoy a land with no restraints. In the evenings he would stop at farmsteads and complete labour in one hour what it would take most men a week to finish.

Randall had been right. With every fresh morning, Milton would wake feeling a little lighter, his lifetime of anger shrinking back down to the root cause. He was certain that by the time he reached the old settlement, his soul would be at peace.

There would be problems, issues, for sure. In the years since Angus' death, the working men had become convinced the outer world had cursed them. Mothers spoke of demons in the woods, and the young children told tales of pixies whispering to them from their bedroom windows. This was all nonsense. But nonsense is hard to shake. Not bound by reason or rules, nonsense creates its own set of laws to suit its agenda. By the time Milton was ready to leave the town for good, the residents of New Bethlehem had built their own religion and there were whispers of destroying the roads into town.

When he reached the roads, he saw the townsfolk had made good on those plans. New Bethlehem had become surrounded by a forest. The old roads had been torn up at the border of the nearest town, a bridge had been burnt, left destroyed as a warning for any unwanted visitors. Milton knew it was a warning for unwanted visitors because next to the remains of the bridge was a sign that said, "No unwanted visitors."

He stopped at the end of the road and grimaced at the trees. He thought of Angus, and the way his mother's face melted into a pool of anguish when she heard the news. Behind him, the nearest town was only a half day's walk away. Kneading the sides of his face with the balls of his palms, he contemplated turning around. Set up shop there for few weeks. Ply his skills.

"Nah," he said, stepping into the woods.

The forest was full of life. None of which he could see. They were busy whistling and chirping and squeaking, hidden in the branches or under the thick mattress of firs he was wading through. It was at this point Milton realised he wasn't carrying a gun. He hadn't needed to for some time. Based on the scraping on the trees, the telltale signs of mating herbivores, it appeared he wouldn't need one.

Milton walked through the heavy flora with a strange sensation. It was as if he were out of breath. He was breathing just fine. Something else, then? His lungs were quivering. There was a light, warm sensation when he inhaled. Was this happiness? No. Excitement? He'd felt pangs of guilt-flecked rapture the first time he met Randall. This was something else. Something deeper. He meandered. His face was aching. Every few steps he would stop to take in the air, to listen to the animals panic and the settle as they forgot about him. He ran his hands across the antler grooves in the trees, wiped his fingers on the dewy leaves and tasted the cold water.

"HABRUH," something yelled. The birds overhead flapped their wings but did not flee the sudden burst of noise. Milton's eyes followed the echoes. It was not an animal sound he recognised. Nor was it a human's voice. At least he hoped not.

"HABRUH."

His head spun. Lurking behind a wide oak tree, a figure about as tall as Milton himself was doing its best to hide.

"Hey there, mister, you from New Bethlehem? I grew up there myself!" Milton waved, trying to be friendly like he'd seen others doing in the past. The figure remained motionless. Milton took a step forward. A twig crack loud beneath his foot.

"HA-HA-PRAAAG!" the figure yelled, running away.

Milton gave chase.

He followed it through the woods until they came to a treeless patch of land. A handful of stone markers stood tall on the ground. He remembered the place from his waking nightmares. It was where he'd found Angus. And the figure had led him there.

Milton charged forwards at the figure. It was running at a jogger's pace, as most large men are wont to do. Milton was a sprinter, though. Always had been. Screaming, the more primeval version of himself, Milton surged forward, and shoulder tackled the figured. They collapsed onto the floor.

"Who are you? Why did you bring me here?"

"PWARB. EEEB. PWARB," the figure said.

Milton inspected the thing he'd been chasing. It was human shaped and covered in a thick ginger fur. Its hands and feet reminded Milton of the gorillas he'd seen with Randall in the city zoo. Its head was the shape of a watermelon, and its face comprised two bulging bug eyes, a tiny, flared nose, massive, brown teeth, and smooth skin. Milton helped it to its feet. It stood looking at him for a moment.

"I know who you are," Milton said through clenched teeth.

"PLERTH."

"You're the beast that killed my brother, ain't you? You ruined my family, you sonofabitch." He swung at the creature; his heavy fist rocked its bulbous head. The blow would have put a smaller man to bed. It stood there caressing its faces, eyes darting from side to side.

"Why did you bring me here!?" he hit the creature again. "Come on, fight. Fight you murderous bastard."

He hit a third, a fourth time. Something snapped as the fifth blow landed on the miniature bridge of the creature's nose. Its face contorted into something evil. It roared and swiped at Milton, sending the man flying into one of the rock pillars. It disintegrated beneath his wait.

Milton lay there catching his breath. He looked at the creature and grinned. "There you are!"

Rushing to his feet he barged into the creature's waiting torso and the two rolled through the dirt exchanging blows and bites. The creature was tough and strong, its hands like metal vices both in terms of grip and sheer force as they slammed into Milton's back. He could feel his bones bend and pop as their tumble took them into a stream. It was clear he would not win on the ground.

Wriggling out of the creature's grip, he returned to his feet and circled his opponent. They were standing in the shallows of a system of rivers. Milton had been trailing the stream right before… He put his fists up, barking at the creature as if it would understand he wanted to go toe to toe. To his surprise, the big-footed beast appeared to understand. It adopted a deep southpaw stance and swung a wild hook at Milton's face. Milton ducked and bobbed, following up with a vicious uppercut-overhand combo. The creature lowered its hands and staggered backward, shaking off the dizziness before returning with a flurry of jabs.

Milton's branchlike forearms absorbed most of the impact. He peaked through the slit between his arms, waiting for an opening. The opening never came. Using a technique Milton had only seen once at a travelling fighting tournament, the creature spun on the ball of its front foot, sending its big rear foot hurtling toward Milton's exposed stomach. The air disappeared from his body within a second and he was thrown some distance down the stream.

He lay there wading in the knee-high water, catching his breath as the creature stomped around the water. "BLAAAAAAARK" it purred. Milton clutched his aching stomach and signalled at the beast, beckoning it to come take another shot. He didn't know why he'd expected the shambling abomination to adhere to standard boxing rules, but since it had no regard for common fist fighting practices, Milton could resort to his own technique. He called it the Closing Time Kata, a method of emptying saloons he's long since perfected on the nights before he met Randall.

The creature came towards his bouncing on the front of its feet, hands swaying side to side with unclenched fists. Milton ran toward it, dodged a snapping front kick, and leapt upward, using the animal's own height for leverage. He fell back to earth forehead first, cracking his diamond-studded skull against the creature's face. It grabbed its nose as the blood gushed, then staggered backwards. Milton did not relent. He followed up with a series of stiff elbows, knees, thumb strikes to the eye sockets.

The creature roared. The whole of the forest called out in response. A cloud of birds formed above the trees and swooped down at Milton. He grasped the giant creature and pulled it down into the waters with him. They rolled and gnashed their teeth and screamed meaningless obscenities at each other while the maelstrom of blackbirds tried to nick at Milton's exposed skin.

They rolled until they reached the first of seven waterfalls. There was no turning back.

The elders of New Bethlehem sat on a small stage in their communal building. Everyone from town was there. It was their harvest meeting. Once a year, one of their children would be chosen to deliver the surplus food to the neighbouring town. This stopped people from asking questions. If the child returned, the town considered them an adult. If not, they became a living part of the forest.

The audience had grown small over the years. The younger folk weren't mating. They'd seen what happened to the older couples. The old men had become drunk, sullen, and remorseful, the women sickly and grey. That was not a future they wanted for themselves, nor a sight they wanted their own children to see. No. Far better to live in service of the surrounding forests.

The older of the eldest elders stood. He was fifty-one years old. He looked over at the town's constituents and tutted.

"We are running out of children for this lottery of ours," he said.

The crowd murmured in agreement.

"I am disappointed in you. As lovely as these young lasses are, not a one of you has thought to get one pregnant. Is it parenthood you fear or what might happen to your progeny? I'll remind you all, we haven't lost a child in seven years. Seven long years. And since then I haven't seen a single one of you ripe and supple young people so much as kiss each other. Just once I'd love to walk around a corner and find two of you locked in an embrace. Annie and Jeff, for instance? How come we haven't seen you two kissing? We've all seen the googly eyes you make. And… but this is none of my business. I'm sorry. I just get carried away. If those of you who haven't delivered the harvest would form a line, we can—"

The side wall shattered as two massive, primitive beasts crashed through it. A frenzied ball of hair and teeth and blood was rolling through the pews of the New Bethlehem community centre. The wooden chairs were bolted to the floor, and yet such was the ire in the fighting animals that they split off from the ground and moved away from the battle. The inhabitants of New Bethlehem retreated to the stage and watched as the blur became two individuals. One they recognised, the other was a venomous, violent man in torn clothes. He revealed his face as he set up; the creature laying prostrate on the floor, convulsing, hands shaking in a pathetic attempt to grab onto something.

They watched in horror as the man rained down a series of blows into the creature's head. He continued until long after the creature had stopped moving. The man looked up at the crowd.

"Milton?" said one elder.

Milton squinted. "Dad?"

"What did you do? Why did you kill our friend?"

Milton looked down at the broken animal, the widening pool of blood. "Friend? No. He killed Angus. He killed Angus. This here's a monster."

His father shook his head. "No, son. This here was the town's guardian. And you killed it. You have to go now."

"But I just got here."

The old man pushed him. "No. Leave now. You've cursed us all, don't you see? You've doomed yourself. The land will grow to hate you. The trees and the flowers, the bear, and the owl, all that exists in this land has become your enemy. If you're fast, you might well escape your fate, but if you stay, you will damn us all. Just as you damned your brother."

Milton squinted. "But I just got here."

The old man pushed him again. "Get out of here. Can't you see we don't want you anymore? Why can't you go back to where you came from?"

Milton looked over his dad's shoulder. He looked confused at the spectral figure who had once been his mother.

"Go!" she said.

"Go!" said everyone.

By Dawn

John rode up to the crest of the hill and looked out at the plains. Even in the twilight, he could see the sparkle of the river, the dark outline of the forest, the patchwork tableau of fields. A shadowy behemoth slithered from east to west. Even with the steam whistles and the billowing plume of grey that clung to it, it was hard to envision. A locomotive. How things had changed. Continued to change. As a boy, he'd slept among half-rotten sacks of meal as a boat trailed laboriously from one side of an ocean to another. Not long after, the bond between man and nature was irrevocably severed. Now metal giants roamed ever outward from cities with factories and concrete tombs full of immigrants. Immigrants like him.

He supposed, for a moment, it was a good thing he was born when he was. The new generation would grow up, some of them, knowing only stone and roads and industry.

Through a set of stolen binoculars, he tried to take a better look at the train. It was little more than a black smudge through the glass. The other riders drew near and squinted to make it out. John pointed at the second last carriage. That much they could make out.

"That metal one near the back is the one we want. Holby and Nash, you two need to take the one behind it and get ready to disconnect it. That's our way out, so do what you have to. The rest of us will head to the third carriage. My guy on the inside said that one's supposed to be empty. We'll make our way through there real quick, get what we came for, and be off before they realise what's happened. By the time they stop that thing, we'll be long gone with the loot."

"You still ain't said what we're looking for," said Holby.

"It's a government train, and that carriage is made of silver and lead. They're keeping all sorts of treasures in there. Don't matter what kind. We'll take what we can, then leave. Simple as that."

"If you say so. Have to get on the damned thing first," Nash said. "Not too keen to be jumping on a train. Never done it before."

"First time for everything, Nash. Besides which, it this thing has half of what they usually do, we'll be curled up in Tahiti by the end of the month."

"Oh, it's Tahiti this week. Thought you had your eye on Mexico?"

"We'll talk about our options later. You all know what we're doing. Keep a clear head. Let's ride!"

John rushed down the slope toward the train, the others following. Nash and Holby split off as planned. John and his associates Joan and Virgil levelled with the side of the third carriage. The train trundled onward, indifferent to its speed, and it took a heavy hand on the horses to keep up with it. Joan and Virgil leapt onto the side of the carriage with surprising ease.

John hesitated. Something was off. A heavy aura. He turned to look for Nash and Holby and saw only their horses. For all his supposed leadership, he was now the last person to jump onto the train. He slowed his horse slightly as he climbed over the saddle and leapt onto the metal steps leading up to the door. His foot slipped and his hands darted for the cold steel bars on either side of him. He let out a hushed laugh so as not to concern his compatriots. They inched toward him as he looked at their prize. A thick metal door, impenetrable to the uninvited, secured by two locks. A wooden warning sign hung above it.

Do NOT Enter:
*Alone
*At Night
*Unarmed

He scoffed briefly before turning his attention to the locks. They'd be simple enough to dismantle if it came down to it.

"What you reckon? Shoot 'em off?" Virgil whispered behind him.

"Not if we can avoid it. Bet the keys are in there."

"Aye," Joan added, "Best avoid any unwanted disturbances until we've got what we've come for."

They entered the third carriage and were met with three men in green uniforms. They were sat at a table playing dominoes, rifles by their sides, and only noticed the invading trio when John's pistol was already aimed at them. They made the usual brief gestures of going for their guns regardless, an unconscious act of trained killers John always enjoyed watching, but paused the Joan and Virgil came into view.

"We don't give one rat's puckered asshole about you three lads, so assuming you all get on the floor real quiet like we can all get off this train in one piece."

The three men obliged. John made to gesture at his accomplices, but they were already hogtieing their new prisoners before his hand so much as twitched. The two of them stood over the prone guards while John searched the room for the keys. The carriage was bare except for the table and a barrel of salted meat in one corner.

"Which one of you's got the keys for those locks, I wonder," John said to the three men.

Two remained silent, but the third, a bearded, older gentleman, was quick to answer. "Oh, you don't want to go in there, bud. I'm not sure what you think is on this train, but it's not here. You can leave us tied up, but you'd be helping us all out if you just jumped off now while you still can."

"No," said John. He took a battered sheet of parchment from his breast-pocket and flapped it in the air. "Bearer bonds, land titles, diamonds, it's all here. And you know what? I think we're taking it all."

"Diamonds? I don't know who sold you that crock of shit, but—"

Virgil's boot found the man's face. He took it as an experienced pugilist would, shaking his head and spitting blood, but with his eyes focused on John. John walked over to him and crouched. He tried to look friendly. His face felt like an overtight mask when he tried to look friendly. He smiled at the man and pointed at the metal door.

"We're getting in there. I would prefer to use the keys and get out of here peacefully, but I'm not above other measures. You got ten seconds, friends. Or one of you leaves through that door yonder."

One of the other guards' eyes bulged, and he stared pleadingly at the older man. John nodded and Virgil lifted the guard up, carrying him to the door. The wind howled outside. The man flailed as best he could against the restraints but was thrown off the train with the same indifference as one would have for a finished apple. If the man screamed, his words were lost among the screams of grinding metal and rushing gusts of air.

"Keys."

Virgil walked over to the other silent guard and lifted him up.

"He's got them. He's got them in his pocket," the guard screamed. Virgil dropped him face first into the ground where he lay whimpering and bleeding in equal measure.

"Gag them," said John before returning his gaze to the older guard. He reached into the man's pockets, searching each one with childlike curiosity until he found the keys. Or rather, key. It was attached to a red placard, the writing illegible to John. "Thanks, friend."

Walking to the metal door, that same dark feeling returned to John as he slid the key into one lock. He ignored it, tossing the useless trinket off the train. The second lock wouldn't give. It needed a second...

"Need this?" a voice came from above him. Nash had climbed over the carriage and was dangling a key just above John's head. "One of the men had it. Did you know this is an army train? I thought we were robbing a bank or something."

John snatched the key and opened the second lock. "You have any trouble back there?"

"There were two army men. I say two. Now there's one. He's pissed. They do not want people going in there."

"Shit, you know what this means, right?"

"No, sir."

"It means we're going to be rich. You head back there and start working on that coupling thing and we'll meet you in a minute."

"Yes sir, can't wait."

Nash disappeared, leaving John alone for a moment to savour opening the thick door. He took in a deep breath and wretched. A stench of old meat and filth engulfed the doorway. Joan and Virgil met him and reacted to the overwhelming stench with the same watery eyed disgust.

From behind them, they could hear the desperate, muffled screams of their captives as entered the carriage. Covering their mouths, they walked into the darkness. The room was sealed off from the outside world. No windows, no vents in the ceiling, no crack of light peeking out from the door across the room. They stood there, just over the threshold, unable or unwilling to move forward.

Joan stepped first. Backward. She retreated briefly to the adjoining carriage and returned with a lantern, but even its dim light could only illuminate so much. It was not a travelling safe, as John led them to believe. There were no signs of bureaucracy in that vessel. The ground was slippery and littered with chicken skin and bones. A few cages hung from the ceiling off of wrought iron hooks. A bookshelf lay toppled on its side, contents torn to shreds, and a small cot lay shattered in the nearest corner.

John didn't need to see any more. "Sorry fellers. Looks like this is some-one's idea of a sick joke. I've gotta apologise because I'm guessing that's all I'm going to be able to give you when the night is through."

Joan nodded along. "I get the first shot at the man who sold you this crock of shit."

"I'm sorry to drag you out here for nothing, Joan."

"Not your fault, John," Virgil said, "This line of work is a gamble. Let's just be thankful we got the drop on those army boys and try better tomorrow."

"I think there's a bank down the tracks a bit. Small town. Probably loaded since it's the middle of the month."

"Yeah, well, let's get off this thing first."

They made it three steps closer to the door before something crashed against the floor in the dark. John turned just in time to see the hunched figure of a giant lumber back into the pitch blackness. A claw flashed out of the shadows and grazed John's cheeked. He backed away, trying to get a better look at it. Joan was already outside, returning to the other carriage, but Virgil was poised as if intending to fight the unknown. In the other carriage, behind Joan, the two bound guards were howling against their gags, muffled screams becoming more desperate with every second.

John backed away further, ready to close the door behind him. "Virg, man, hurry up!" he hollered. "I'll lock you in there!"

Virgil turned. "Just a mom—" he said, interrupted by a scaly black mass that enveloped his head entirely. For an instance it seemed as if he was half lost in shadows, but then the unhinged maw of whatever lurked in there with him let go revealing what remained of his body. Virgil, or at least Virgil from the collarbone down, stood there for a moment, too confused to know he was already dead. His heart had yet to learn the truth as it continued to pump two jets of deep red blood up to the ceiling.

Even as the man's headless remains fell to the ground John was closing the door. He held it shut and searched his pockets for the locks before remembering he'd chucked them off the train. He eyed the ground on either side of him, but the train was gathering speed and a jump promised only a brief escape and a slow death. It was unclear if this was a preferable way to end things.

Joan grabbed him and tried to force him to one side, reaching for the door's wheeled handle. "We've got to save him!" she called out. "We've got to kill it!"

John gripped her hand and held it, looking into her eyes until the fire within cooled. "There's nothing we can do now except get off this thing."

They climbed atop the metal container and crawled across the roof. The creature inside was wide away, banging against the sides with impotent rage. They could hear its bellows even above the whistling air that threatened to carry them off the train and to their deaths.

"I curse the day these things were invented," John shouted, his voice lost in the pandemonium.

Reaching the other side, they came to the ladder just in time to find Nash standing beside an open door. He looked at them, befuddled. "What kept you so long?" he asked.

In response, the beast leapt out of the shadows and caught Nash in its massive mouth. They could see more of it, albeit a blurred and frenzied mass of chaos as it tore into the poor Nash. A lumbering creature, both human and not. It wore the tattered remains of an officer's uniform, but its skin was rigid and green. Its head was that of an alligator, that ancient and perfect instrument of death.

John watched awestruck for all of a second before Joan unloaded her weapon into the stiff hide of the creature. It was unfazed. Holby had been grinning mere moments before, but stood inches away from the evisceration. He looked at his fellow robbers, mouth agape, eyes lost of all reason. He snapped out of it and grabbed a rifle from the ground and rushed to the steel door that had just doomed Nash.

"The cut bar! Shoot the damn cut bar!"

"Huh?"

"Disconnect the carriage!"

John and John climbed back up to the roof of the carriage while Holby fiddled with his rifle. And aimed it at the bars between the carriage. It was a rough angle. He shifted and repositioned himself a dozen times, trying to remove the rear carriage without endangering himself. All the while, the creature devoured Nash, leaving only a mound of mush and tattered clothing on the ground. It spun to find Holby sitting with his back to it and pounced.

The rear carriage shuddered and broke away from the rest of the train. It took with it the lower half of Holby. His torso had been torn off by the creature moments after uncoupling the platforms.

John was lost to panic. He looked once again at the darting figures of the passing terrain and thought hard about jumping. Three good men had died in what felt like ten seconds because of his impulses. It was only fair he die to. He thought. It would be so easy to let go. To fall. Immediate penance.

Joan watched his face fade into the realms of self-pity as they clung to the sides of the train. "No," she said. "You don't get to leave me here."

"You could jump too. We could make it."

"No. I'm not dying until that thing is dead, and neither are you. Sack up and follow me."

Joan lifted herself onto the roof and walked with the grace of a circus performer to the next carriage. Try as he might, John could not replicate this, looking instead like a punch-drunk wino trying to follow a simple set of instructions. Namely: don't fall off the moving train. Beneath them, the alligator man had tired once again of its prey and could be heard sniffing out another meal.

By the time John had reached what was the third carriage, Joan was already trying to untie the guards.

"Hold up," John said, panting as he climbed down the ladder and into the chamber. "We untie those guys, they'll get the others."

"Yes," Joan replied.

"Ungag them first. Need to make sure they won't do anything stupid."

"There's a walking crocodile chasing after us, I think self-preservation will buy us a few minutes. Ain't that so?" She removed the stuffing from the bearded man's mouth. He was soaked in cold sweat and his skin had become dotted with red spots from his efforts to escape.

"What the hell did you's do?" he asked. "It's going to kill us all!"

"Oh, come on," John replied. "It's not like it can work that door."

It worked on that door. Metal squealed as the handle spun from inside. The hinges creaked, the alligator man roared, the prisoners screamed. The four of them stared as the door pushed open, a claw the size of a cat wrapped around one side. It was the sight of the claw that prompted a rediscovered need to escape. Both bound men wriggled across the floor, the bearded man barking obscenities while the other could only expel muffled nothings.

Joan tried to fire at the beast as it emerged from its prison, but her chambers had long since run out of bullets. Her hammer clacked pathetically against her gun. She turned and crouched once more to help the tied men but John, in his eagerness to leave, lifted her up by the elbow and marched her into the adjoining carriage. She jostled with him until it was clear the creature was in the room.

It walked with deliberate, predatory steps, slow and cold-blooded. Sinewy clumps of three dead men's flesh hung from its back teeth. The green uniform it was wearing was coated in layers of dark stains. It looked at them with dead yellow eyes, with an indifference that made them clamour for savagery, anything but the blank stare of death incarnation.

"Sorry," Joan said to the prone men.

"Wait! No. YOU FUCKING WAIT! You're not leaving us with this thing! You can't! You can't!" the bearded man yelled after them while they opened a door and entered the next carriage.

A young boy was fiddling with a fine violin in the centre of the carriage. It was a bright stretch of wooden boards, bunk beds, and lanterns. Five men in uniform sat around the dancing boy, stomping their feet and clapping one hand against their chest while they swung tankards of beer above their heads. The boy dropped his fiddle at the sight of John and Joan, and the five men continued to chant and celebrate until it became obvious he was screaming. They turned, almost at once, and saw the two bandits standing in the doorway. Scrambling for their weapons, they barked orders at the two interlopers until it became clear it was not them the fiddler was screaming at.

The bearded man, hands still fastened to his ankles, was swinging violently in the air, stomach enveloped by the beast's clenched mouth. On the floor beside the carnage, the other man was bashing his exposed skull against the wall in one last attempt at escape.

"Lose that carriage immediately," one guard barked.

"And set it loose in the wild?"

"It'll come to its senses in the morning. Now shut up and do it."

Two men rushed to loosen the bar connecting the carriages as the hisses and screams and sounds of rending flesh filled the air. They kicked at the metal, tugging at it. Something was jammed.

"And do something about these two, god dammit," the guard said.

As instructed, another man waved his pistol at John and Joan and marched them to the rear of that carried. They walked backward, not wanting to take their eyes off either the gun or the living manifestation of doom careening ever closer toward them.

Cheers as the guards uncoupled the carriage. Its momentum waned, and it slowed behind them. Their celebrations were short-lived. The creature, noticing the ebb in speed, dropped the still-twitching meal of his and surged forward, leaping high into the air. It vanished, for a moment, in the darkness, but announced it was still there with a loud thud as it landed hard on the ceiling. The guards aimed their guns up at the thumping, waiting for the right moment to shoot. John and Joan's man turned away from them and joined the others.

Joan watched as the men formed a circle and aimed their weapons upward. They all jolted as claws tore into the ceiling and ripped off a section. Without waiting for instruction, the men opened fire. John tugged at her elbow. The men raced to reload, which gave the creature enough time to reach down and grab a man's head. He screamed as the hand hoisted him up through the hole, but the screams were short-lived, replaced by yelling and gunfire.

John tugged hard, forcing Joan into the last carriage. It was like walking into a new train entirely.

They were in a sleeper carriage. The walls were lit up by candelabras, revealing the ivory wallpaper and rich mahogany lining. Two people in formal attire stood in their doorways. They were unfazed by the sounds coming from the rear carriage.

"You two," one of them said, "I thought we'd agreed you'd all keep to the back and not disturb us."

John coughed and did his best to appear as an underling. "Uh yeah, sure, pardon to bother you all, but there's a giant walking alligator on the loose back there and it's killing everyone."

He pushed by them. Joan followed, still looking over her shoulder. Not out of concern, but a need to be proactive. The two aristocrats sighed and muttered and appealed to their superior status, but it was no good. John walked to the last room in the carriage and slammed his fist against the door. It opened. Inside was a portly man in a vest and suspenders. He'd covered his hairy chest in churned butter and was holding a portrait of an English monarch.

"My word," the man said through his jowls, "What is the meaning for this disturbance?"

"We need your room," said John, yanking the man out. He landed on the floor and sat there dumbfounded while John ushered Joan into the room. The door locked in his face. Unlocking and reopening briefly so that John could hand him the rest of his supplies.

"You get out of my room!" the man yelled.

John leaned against the door, almost laughing at the man's limp slaps. The knocks became furious, carried by the indignation of a man too convinced of his own superiority.

Joan glared at John.

"What's the matter?"

"You're a chickenshit. We're all going to die because you got no balls."

"That so? What would you have me do? Stick around to help the guys who'd turn around and kill us next? Should I let that old pervert in his room?"

"Please do," the man whimpered outside.

Joan began searching the room for something to use. "I just thought you were some brave leader when I signed up, is all. Forget that, I thought you had a plan. A vague semblance of one, at least. All you've done tonight is get a bunch of people killed."

The knocking and yelling outside became screaming. Joined by three more sets of hands. They pleaded for help as the creature thudded down the carriage, hissing, roaring as it approached them.

"Damn you for a thousand lifetimes," someone screamed. Their voice then became a bloodcurdling series of nothings. John slumped against the door. Listening to the feast behind the door, the sounds of tearing flesh and muscle. He could feel his pants dampen as blood ooze through the slit beneath the door. He looked up at Joan.

"You know a little secret," he said to her. "Brave men don't last too long. That's why I'm here and the other three aren't. All we have to do is wait until dawn. You heard what that man said. We wait until dawn and everything will be fine."

"Unless it forces its way in here. Or we get to a town and it kills all those people. How many deaths are you comfortable with?"

"So long as they ain't mine."

Joan shook her head. She cracked open the window and squeezed through, poking her head through the gap just long enough to give John one last disapproving look.

John stood up. The stains on his pants made him feel sick. As did the sounds coming from just outside the door. Someone was still banging against it, weakly, as their body was moved from one side to the other by the ravenous creature. John covered his face with his hands and tried not to listen. The blood on the floor was expanding across the carpet. John tried not to look. He tried not to look. Even with his ears covered he could hear the lip-smacking feeding frenzy in the corridor. It was all his fault. He tried not to listen. The window was open still, the cold air from outside blew on his neck, his neck was damp and overheating. Opening his eyes, the room was a coagulated blur, his eyes cursed with a new photosensitivity, so the weak lights shone like stars and everything else faded into swirling mist. The outside world of sounds was submerged beneath an unrelenting high-pitched squeal. His knees were weak. He couldn't feel his limbs. Trying to move forward he couldn't tell is he was slipping on the blood or if the train was moving up a steep incline. Everything was off. Everything was over. His reactions were delayed. It was like his consciousness was shrinking every downward into the core of his being. He reached for the dead pervert's bed and tried to pull it down, but his arms were not his own. All muscles had abandoned him. How could he fight an alligator-man if he couldn't even wrestle a small bed out of the wall? He tugged. He tugged. It fell into place, and then so did he.

For what could have been an hour, his soul wafted through an unfamiliar, violet-hued world. People in suits walking across marble floors. Blinding light pouring in out of giant windows. The sounds of a new world coming to him all at once, like a diver returning to the surface.

He woke up and wasn't sure where he was. A hotel? His jaw was sore. He'd chipped a tooth by the feel of things. Tongue licking over newly jagged edges. His limbs were his again, but had atrophied. No. Not a hotel. A train. There was a—

The upper section of the door exploded as a clawed hand forced its way through.

There was something else, too. Muffled shouting. John recollected himself as best he could and looked at the window. Joan had returned. She was desperate.

"John, get your ass up now. I need your help to get out of here or we're both dead. Hurry, man."

He stood and was reminded all too fast how closed the claw was to him as it swiped his arm, tearing open his shirt and his bicep. Recoiling, he rolled to the window and pulled himself up. Joan offered no help. His senses were still returning, and he strained to listen to her.

"Out here," she said, giving him her hand.

He could barely hold on to the side of the train as it rocked forward. They were approaching a bridge, by the looks of it. Joan had climbed up to the roof, but John couldn't find the strength to follow her.

"That's fine, John, you stay down there."

"What's the plan?"

"I need you to go back to the guard—"

The creature had burst into the sleeper room. John found his strength to climb up to the roof. They lay there in silence.

Joan whispered, "I need you to get back to the guard carriage, lure that bastard back there, and then meet me up front. We can ride the engine car for a few miles. Controls don't look too hard and failing anything else we can just overheat the engine."

"Uncoupling hasn't worked yet."

"If that doesn't work, we have enough time to drive off the bridge if we have to."

"That'd kill us."

"Big whoop. Meet me back up front. Hurry."

John crawled along the roof to the rear carriage. It seemed like only a minute ago he'd entertained dreams leading a band of desperados, running roughshod across the country. He couldn't even rob a train. What he could do, he thought, was safe at least one person. Maybe Joan would have better luck with her own gang. She had the aptitude for it.

John dropped through the hole in the guard's carriage and landed on the entrails and broken bones of the guards they'd abandoned. He was numb to it, even as the edge of a rib carved its way into his hand. He stood there. The creature was roving in the affluent carriage, oblivious for the time being.

"Hey!" John shouted. He waited for the creature to hear him. "Hey!" he called again. It turned.

John remained motionless. The creature bounded towards him, and he flung his hands to the side and kept his eyes open. It would buy Joan more than enough time. The creature leapt on him and instead of relying on its enormous mouth, played with his stomach. Exploratory slices at first. Small gashes appearing on his chest. John didn't even scream. In fact, he laughed.

He laughed as the creature carved the skin from his flesh and he laughed as Joan disconnected the engine from the rest of the train and road off to safety on her own. The carriage sped up and jack-knifed as it reached the bridge.

At least he was right about the bridge.

Flying for a second, John was amazed the creature would fall so far and yet refuse to let go of him. They landed in a shattered heap together on the riverbed. The train exploding all around them. It was only upon impact the creature let go.

Flames made fast work to devour the oil-laden joints and lacquered wood. The riverbed was lit up by the fire as it laid claim to the remains of the train. John lay there on a boulder and watched as the creature slunk off into the night.

"Hey!" he called again.

"Hey, you come back and you kill me."

"Kill me, damn you!"

A weak hiss as the creature vanished into the deeps of the river. John lay furious on the ground, with only his pain and the fire for company.

"Hey!" he called. He called and called. Until the sun rose and set again.

That Glitters

Foreman George wobbled as he climbed on his seat. The others didn't notice. Just as well. Cupping his mouth with both hands, he yelled a few random syllables. It was only because he was paying them that the five mercenary miners stopped to look at him. They were loyal men, to a point, sworn to secrecy with the promise of more gold than they could comprehend, much less spend in one lifetime.

There was an old shaft just up the hill. It had stood there abandoned for a half century. Those long-dead prospectors, foolish coots to a man, had given up mere inches too soon. At least that was the hope. A giant vein lay waiting for them down below, unmolested and plentiful. By the rough estimate of rumour multiplied by greed, George would have enough to survive five hundred years. More still if his men succumbed to tragic, unavoidable accidents in the near future.

The men were sitting around a table in the ramshackle waystation at the foot of the mountain. Its floorboards were bent, nails gnarled upwards like waiting snakes. Ceiling cracked upon by age and elements. Windows boarded up. This was to be their life for several weeks. The six of them with only each other for company.

George had worked with the two oldest men before. Malachi and Winston were honourable, honest, hardworking men he'd met in the northeast. It was the other three he was less sure about. Pickings were slim, though, so he'd been forced to depend on what presented itself as available. Richter, at the very least, came with an old friend's recommendation. Joshua and Mordecai, however, had nobody to vouch for them, and only their doe-eyed quest for hard work had convinced George to take them on. That and the fact that not only did young workers fail to understand the true meaning of a decent wage but were also the easiest to blame should someone get crushed to death.

But anyway, the men were looking at George with shrinking eyes.

"Lads," he said, flashing his brown teeth, "You best drink up and drink up well for we shall spend the near future underground or sleeping. First, we must check the beams and support columns. This here's an old mine and we don't need it collapsing on us until we're good and ready. But I am certain to say we shall be rich by month's end. All we have to do is work hard and work smart. What says ye!?"

The men all cheered in their own particular ways. George made a quick study of each of them: Malachi, Richter, and Mordecai whooped with the half-assed noise of veteran sots who'd much rather be drinking; Winston grumbled a single "yup" and twiddled his thumbs; Joshua forced a toothy aberration of a smile and mimed along. Him. He would be the one. George knew it the instant their eyes met, and the boy looked down at his boots. Joshua would take the fall, and everyone would buy it. Of course the weak, pusillanimous waif would mess up. It was only a matter of time. George raised a glass to his own good fortune; he'd been gifted a patsy without even trying.

With the future set in stone, George revealed a gift he'd been hiding. A barrel of whiskey he'd had brought up the day before, hidden under a pile of coarse sheets. The miners roared once more at the sight of the thing and set upon it like Badlands coyotes. They all drank freely, and before long George found himself grateful there were no guns or women in the vicinity. Those more carnal celebrations he'd reserve for himself.

The night wore on. Drinking turned to sipping and superficial conversations became empty words. Winston fell asleep in his chair, fingers interlinked on his protruding stomach. The rest of them played liar's dice. They played with a familiarity toward each other only liquor could produce. George for his part played along, but the true game of the room existed only inside his mind.

Richter had taken to betting too big too fast on the dice, trapped as he was by the need to prove his manliness. He'd been eliminated first three games in a row and had taken to slamming his cup on the table. A sore loser. George almost felt bad for the man.

"Richter, my man, the night is still young. You keep giving yourself away like that and we're going to run out of things to play. Didn't no one bring no dice nor nothing?"

"Huh? I don't even like this game. Always was a poor liar," Richter said. He looked down at his remaining die. "Alright, I got five threes."

Mordecai raised a hand. "Ah, in vino veritas! Five fours."

Malachi's head bobbed while he did the math in his head. His fingers twitched. "Ha. Et in Arcadia ego! Five sixes."

"Tempus fugit," Mordecai replied.

"What the blazes are you fellers blabbering about now? I thought we was playing dice?" Richter said.

George guffawed. He looked like a proud rooster. "Well, son, I'd say these two were educated men. They's speaking Latin, boy. The tongue of the scholar."

"And now there're tongues involved? What is going on?"

"Richter, relax," Joshua said. He had been silent the whole night unless announcing his bets. "They're quoting stock phrases like it means something. Nothing too impressive. I'd wager neither one could recite Pliny or Tacitus."

"Who?"

"Exactly. Ille tenet palmam, palma petenda mea ist."

They collectively winced in Joshua's direction. Even Winston sputtered and seemed to shake his head.

"Nevermind," said the boy, "I have six sixes."

"Then I done reckons you're a liar, Joshua."

Joshua smiled. "Indeed. But not this round."

They lifted their cups to reveal their dice. There were seven sixes in play. Joshua had three of them. Not a single four could be seen. George tossed a sacrifice to the loser's pile and sipped his drink. Perhaps he'd have to reconsider Joshua.

In the morning they made their first trip into the mine equipped with sore heads and lamps. It was not far beneath the surface and they needed only to walk down a slight slope. The hole was wide, filled with the scars of hard work. Despite being abandoned, the wood was tight, secure, almost still alive at it propped up the ceiling. As they wandered in deeper, there were a few exploratory holes dug in the sides, a few stacks of chiselled rock left as unwanted mementos of a failed venture.

The inner pit was marked by a sudden drop in the ground. The six men staggered down into the chamber and looked at the grooves in the wall. From down there, the sunlight from outside could not be seen. George had them all blow out their lamps, and they stood there beneath the world. It was like a tomb a pharaoh would find themselves in, with just as much wealth nearby. The ceiling glimmered in the darkness, small shards of minerals radiating back from the memories of the lantern. It looked almost as if they were standing beneath an open sky on some strange land.

"It's dark," said Richter.

George had tried to dig out the treasure for himself several months earlier. It had not been an easy endeavour. He'd extracted just enough gold to pay for supplies and attract his new crew. There in the dark he walked over to where he remembered digging and turned his light back on. The gold was still there, smiling at them, winking suggestively, hidden behind a thin layer of earth. The other five joined him beside the glow of his lantern and stared like love-struck schoolboys at the riches waiting for them.

For the rest of the first week they worked in constant shifts, seldom leaving the mine unattended. Mordecai, Richter, and Joshua worked through the nights to the limp Geordie light hanging above them. With every swing of their picks they grew more confident, fast adapting to their work. George watched over Malachi and Winston as they dug from dawn until dusk. In the evenings, for a half hour, the six of them would sit around a table. The elders would drink and share stories of the north-east while the groggy younger miners wolfed down their breakfasts. Never again would all six of them enjoy a night of gaming and drinking.

Time in the mine was gruelling and suffocating; time, in fact, lost all meaning in that darkened pit. A minute and an hour soon felt like the same thing, and even the brief relief of sleep became another plunge into sore darkness.

The gold, low, was finding its way out of the holes. This was all the motivation the six men required. Whenever the welts on their palms ached or the lower part of their back felt fused together, all they had to do was admire the growing collection of gold.

On the sixth day, Joshua noticed his fellow novices had begun to speak in code. They would chip away at the lode and palm small nuggets for themselves, referring to "Polly" and "Lady Genevieve" and other fictional relatives. Then there were the nods and winks and nudges they performed right in front of him. He wasn't angry they didn't want to invite him to take part in their subterfuge, but their brazenly low opinions of his intellect were insulting. He tried his best to ignore them, swinging away at the rocks until the alarm bell rang for the end of their shift. It was at the end of the shift when Richter winked at Mordecai, who pretended to have forgotten something in the mine.

"You're too quiet not to trust," Richter said. "I know you've clocked on to us, and it's been six days you've had the chance to report us to George. I think we should let you in on it."

"I don't care if you're stealing a little," said Joshua. "I don't need much money."

"No, you misunderstand. We mean to take everything."

"Oh. And how are you going to do that? I think they'd probably notice the missing gold."

"Well, see, we don't imagine there's more than but two or three days left of digging at this rate and those shafts in there are mighty old. I mean, surely there'll collapse any day now. You'll know when. Just thought you should know. You seem like an alright kid."

"And what's in this for me, then?"

"Just your life, Joshua. Ain't no amount of gold worth that. You're welcome."

Joshua nodded. "Indeed. Thank you, my friend. This has been most illuminating."

"What? Oh, huh, sorry, I'll turn the lamp off. And but anyway, besides all that, dollars to biscuits, these old-timers are planning something far worse. So keep your eyes peels, OK?"

Joshua let out an offended sigh. "They would never!"

Joshua knew exactly what Ol' George's plans were. He knew following night, just before the start of his shift, George would take him outside for "constructive feedback" only to then request that Joshua covertly feed a line of detonating chord down a specially, diligently grooved line on the left wall of the shaft. Joshua knew this just as he knew the fate of the mine, the miners, and the gold, because Joshua knew most things.

And when George pulled him to one side to "chat about digging techniques" Joshua listened like a schoolboy and agreed with the mock reluctance of a spineless follower. He made a point of clumsily collecting the hidden spool, of struggling to unwind it, knowing full well George was inside the waystation laughing at him.

What came next, however, almost surprised Joshua as much as it did George, Richter, and Mordecai. The entire week, and the months prior, Malachi and Winston had been concocting plans of their own. When the three night workers stirred from their exhausted slumber, they were startled by the crash of George's head slamming into the ground. He lay there whimpering, clutching his bent and bloody nose. His eyes were swelling even as he stared at the three sleeping youngsters. Malachi and Winston stood over them, tall, proud, and overconfident, as is often the case with armed men in control of the defenceless.

"Time for one last dig, boys," Winston laughed, cocking his shotgun, and swinging it in the air. The sleepers were still wiping the crud from their eyes, still trying to understand what was happening. He fired into the ceiling. "Now."

The disgruntled, beaten George shuffled ahead of the others as they were marched into the mine. A chorus of questions and curses left his lips and echoed over the hill to an audience of zero. "You damned fools," he whistled through his cracked teeth. "How are you getting the gold back to town if it's just the two of ye?"

"Same ways you was planning, most likely," Malachi guffawed. "Now keep that split mouth of yours shut unless you want to eat a bullet. In fact, you all best be quiet. Next one to talk gets shot."

"What if we need your help with something?" Joshua asked.

The answer came in the form of a bullet. Joshua fell, clasping his chest. Malachi booted him until his body rolled down the hill toward the waystation. The others stopped, mouths agape, until the butt of Malachi's pistol slammed into the back of Richter's head. They all remembered how to walk then.

The three unarmed men dug like they were digging graces. They would heft chunks of gold into the rusted mine cart and try not to look at anything but the work at hand. Malachi and Winston were enjoying their flasks of liquor and seemed eager to hit someone. The taste of blood does that to a man. Winston laughed and swished the whiskey in his mouth, swallowing with a satisfied smack of his lips. "You all thought you were so smart, didn't you? All planning to rob each other. And now look at you."

Malachi echoed this sentiment. "Think you're so smart," he would say after every belt of tequila.

Mordecai was the first to break down and plead for his life, knowing full well the time was almost at hand. For his troubles, Winston rammed his steel-toed boot into the boy's stomach and forced the tip of his shotgun between his lips. "Can I? We only need two at this stage," he said, looking at Malachi.

"All the same to me," Malachi replied.

"I'd be careful firing that down here," a voice called out from the mouth of the tunnel. "Last thing you want is a cave in." Footsteps. A man walked into the weak light of the lanterns. Joshua stood with his hands on his hips. The others were too preoccupied to notice, but he had changed his clothes to a tailored suit.

Mordecai pointed his gun at him. "Was one bullet not enough to convince you to stay down."

"Amicus, you don't have enough bullets to convince me to do anything."

"I don't know about that, lad."

The two armed fools aimed at Joshua. Even in the dim light, they could see the glint of his teeth as his mouth formed a smile. His eyes flashed as he spoke with a level of detachment not one man in the pit had heard before. "Just remember that I'm serious about the cave in. Shoot."

They obliged. With a drumroll of gunfire, they unloaded their guns at the grinning buffoon. Their blasts knocked Joshua back into the darkness. Winston looked up at the rocks above them. "So much for that," he laughed.

They turned their attention to the three diggers. All three of them were standing now, knowing for sure the two guns were empty. As the guns hit the floor and hands rolled into fists, something shuffled in the darkness.

"Sorry," came Joshua's voice. "My count was a little off. The cave-in happens now." A heavy exhalation as something slammed into a supporting beam. The ceiling rumbled, clumps of dirt and rock fell. The sunlight from the outside world vanished forever as the only way out of the bit was buried behind a wall of debris. The lanterns sputtered and died, and yet the room remained illuminated. Each wall, the floor, was made of a glimmering gold the likes of which none had seen before. The veiling glowed with celestial beauty.

They all but forgot they were buried alive. Joshua stood leaning against where the entryway had been, arms folded, wearing the face of a serial adulterer who would never get caught. He unfolded his arms and presented the treasures to his fellow men.

"Do you see? All the gold in the world for you five!"

Winston stepped forward and pointed his shotgun at Joshua's head. "I've had enough of you. Time to die."

Joshua waved him off. "Not for me. Besides, you're out of bullets, old timer. It's a shame I can't stay here. This home you've built for yourselves is going to be home to some interesting stories."

George laughed, flecks of blood splashing out from his mouth. "You're a damned fool. You're trapped down here with us!" He looked at the others. "And you're all fools too. We could have discussed this like gentlemen. Now we all get to die down here because of your greed!"

"I'm not," Joshua shook his head.

"Blathering nincompoop, you're stuck down here with the rest of us."

The glimmer of the gold dulled, the marvellous ceiling above became black, and they were submerged forever in darkness. There was no telling who was the first to scream as their voices sounded the same.

"I'm not down there," said Joshua.

And he wasn't.

Dead Hand

John stood at one end of town awaiting salvation. None was to come. Milton strode like a forgotten titan over the white sand and stood proud some distance away. Joshua lingered in the saloon's doorway and watched like a magpie searching for a new prize.

"You best shoot true," John yelled. His voice carried over the sands.

"I aim to," Milton replied.

"Ha! Then draw!"

And draw Milton did. Faster than a man of his size had any right to. John hadn't even made a show of reaching for his gun. Milton emptied the chambers of his gun and each bullet struck John's exposed chest. John was beaten backwards by the impact and he flipped in the air before crashing to the ground. Milton holstered his weapon and walked toward his fallen opponent.

"I'm sorry it came to that," he said as he walked by Joshua.

Drawing near the body, he could hear breathing. John's limbs twitched, convulsed, then pressed down on the ground. He stood up and looked down at his ruined body where the bullets landed. Nothing. Not a single speck of blood on his person.

"What in the world?" Milton said.

John ran his hands across his body, not believing he was unharmed. At first he appeared confused, but that confusion quickly turned to anger. "You were supposed to kill me! I'm supposed to die!" John stomped his feet, gnashed his teeth, and clenched his first while Milton could only mutter useless apologies.

"You damn fool!" John cried out, snatching at his own weapon. He fired twice at Milton, who obligingly died, the top of his enormous head torn off by the impact.

John fell back down to his knees and continued to stare at his absence of injuries. He shot Milton's body two more times and then turned the gun on himself, opening his mouth and firing two blasts into his mouth. He coughed and gagged and spat. The spit contained clumps of molten lead, but no blood.

"I'm supposed to die here!" He sat there and tried to cry.

"I told you, John," Joshua Cross said from the doors of the saloon. "I told you I would be the one to kill you. This is an unalterable fact all of nature must now observe. You can and you will try to prove me wrong in time, but you will die by my hand when the time is right."

He walked toward John with a glib indifference, stopping for a moment to pay his respects to the fallen Milton.

"What have you done to me?"

"Nothing you don't deserve, I'm sure. How many people have died because of you? How many friends? I've known of your misadventures for some time. Just as I knew all about Alfredo and Milton here." He chuckled. "And I guess, since I'm being honest, I knew all about the mayor of this town too."

"Is that your game? Divine retribution?"

Joshua lifted John to his feet. He turned him around and pointed at a dark mass in the distance. A convoy was coming. Above them the sky was black with carrion birds. "Divine? Barely. I need help with something, and you were an ideal candidate."

"And the others?"

"Well, if I must be honest, and I must be, I was hoping Milton would come around. But he was too honest for his own good. Shame. You know he once fought a… but we'll get to that. As for Alfredo, I needed to send a message."

"To the Lawman."

"Yes!" Joshua beamed. "Yes, you're figuring it out properly now. There are men who mean to end me, John, and I need you to bring them to me."

John watched the cloud of crows and buzzards draw close. There were so many they all but blotted out the sun. Approaching them on foot was a travelling circus of sorts. Twisted depictions of performers painted on the side of wagons. Caged animals and people alike kept in cages. The riders wore painted skull masks and were accompanied by violinists and organ players performing from within a stagecoach.

"And if I don't help you?"

"That's up to you, my friend. You'll grow tired of being alive, eventually. We all do. And to be honest, maybe you should get right with yourself first? Travel a little? Make it up to Joan's family. Whatever you want. I'm not an evil man, John. You won't be forced into anything you don't want to do."

A coach pulled along by two chestnut horses stopped beside them. The rider was dressed as a carnival barker. Joshua climbed up the coach's steps and open the door. Inside was decked with a resplendent red velvet. Bottles of water and spirits, platters full of grapes and strawberries, a pipe that filled the air with a familiar smell. They were all waiting in there. John gave pause.

"What's the matter, John?"

"Nothing, just thought the horses would be white is all."

"They were. But I thought it a little on the nose. We're authors of our own destiny now, John. Get in."

They got in. John sank into the velveteen chair waiting for him and could feel his restless, sinful spirit dissipate. He inhaled the sweet smells of the moving box and closed his eyes. "These men you're after…"

Joshua lit the pipe and gulped at the stem, holding a thick smoke in his lungs for a moment before exhaling. "I'm going to tell you about two men who want me dead. One is a fool who wants revenge. His foolishness makes his thirst all that more dangerous. They other… well, he's a man of a different type. He hasn't even learned he wants to kill me yet, but he will soon enough. And when he does, my friend, we must be ready."

"Uh… that's all very vague and all, but how am I to help?"

"We'll get to that. But first. Try the grapes. Maybe an apple. It's all exceptionally good."

Shang-High Noon

The Lawman stroked his new horse's cheek. It was a piss poor horse, skittish, near incontinent, and reluctant to press on but. It needed constant reassurance. All around them, the servile class was working in groups of five or six, swinging pickaxes, carting off rubble, laying metal girders, all in the name of progress. He nodded approvingly at them. It was good when people knew their station, which coincidentally was what they were building.

He walked through the workers to the beginnings of a wooden staircase. A man better dressed than the others was looking over a set of plans, instructing the more Aryan of his underlings on what to do next. The Lawman walked toward him.

"Uh-huh?" the foreman said, not taking his eyes off the blueprints.

The Lawman stood straight so that everyone might see his size. He took his billfold from his pocket and spoke as deeply as he could. "I am looking to buy a worker off you."

The foreman moved his head briefly and returned to his work. "Oh yeah? You don't look like you work railroads, bud."

"That's because I don't. I am a man of Law. I'll pay good money."

"Why didn't you say so? Take your pick."

"Well, that's just the thing. I've heard rumours one of your men is a legendary sword fighter and I was hoping you could point him out to me."

"A sword fighter? You know there're guns now, right? But, uh, sure, sure, we can figure something out."

The Lawman put his billfold back in his pocket and his hand returned with two coins of Mayan gold. "Would this be sufficient?"

"Naw, my men are closer to four coins, would be my estimate. What do the rest of you say?"

His cohorts mumbled their agreements.

"As you wish," said the Lawman, placing four coins on the table. "Now that's settled, I am looking for the one they call Oo-Shai."

"Ooh-wha? Oh! Oh, aye, sure thing, boss," the foreman was grinning. "Yeah, he's in the canteen. Keeps to himself. Best of luck with that. Now if you'll excuse us."

They returned to their map.

Even a moment of motionless was enough to succumb to the humidity. The Lawman's leather's tightened against his skin as he tried to spot the canteen. It was out there. The largest tent on the other side of the half-finished railroad. Rows of tables surrounded a central grill. Groups of iterant workers kept to their own kind and swarmed the benches en masse, gorging themselves on stewed beef and tepid water. Men from all lands were represented beneath that canvas roof, but the Lawman, in his infinite wisdom, knew exactly where to go.

He walked to where the Chinamen were eating. They seemed to own their own tract of the canteen. Most were huddled together, yelling nonsense at each other and smacking their gums while they ate. One man sat alone, the other workers no doubt intimidated by his brave aura. The legendary Oo-Shai himself. With a limp toss, he aimed a Mayan coin at the man's lap. It landed with a weak donk. The Lawman crouched beside him.

"I've been searching for you, Oo-Shai. I have a very important job for you."

"Not now, I'm on a break." Oo-Shai spoke more clearly than the Lawman expected. To an untrained ear, he would have sounded drunk. The Lawman knew better.

"It's not that kind of job, my friend." The Lawman flicked another coin at him.

"Come a long way out to nowhere for sexual favours, ain't ya?"

Another coin. "Nothing like that. I need your help with an important task. I've bought your freedom."

"Oh! Why didn't you say so? Where are we going?"

They walked outside to the Lawman's waiting horse. "I'm glad I found you so easily, Oo-Shai. Time is of the essence. Do you have your legendary sword with you? Or will any sword do?"

"Sword? What are you talking about? I'm a railroad worker."

"But you are Oo-Shai."

"My name's Bobby Jiaolong, champ."

"Then where's Oo-Shai?"

"There's no way that's an actual name, big man. Who told you he'd be here?"

The Lawman handed over the parchment he'd been given, and Bobby Jiaolong spoke aloud as he read it. He read it twice. He scrunched his eyes and looked back into the mess hall. "Right, well, see, you've made a slight mistake, but I know what you've done."

"Great. Now if you'll just point me to the great Oo-Shai, you can get back to your break."

"Yeah… no, that will not happen, big boy. I'll take you to your man on one condition."

"Don't try a man of the Law, boy."

"Your threats might work with office clerks, but I don't care. Do you want to meet your friend or not?"

The Lawman clenched his teeth and whistled, "Sure."

"Great! So you've got to agree to take me too. And pay me five more of these coins. Then I'll help you."

The Lawman handed him another stack of coins and followed him back under the tent. Bobby walked him to the Chinese table. The Lawman looked at each worker with an appraiser's eye. But Bobby was still walking. He walked to the far end of the tent and stopped beside a dishevelled and gaunt Irishman. The man sat cross-legged and deep in a trance.

The Lawman stared at the man's Hibernian features, his red hair and blistered pale skin. There was no way he was Chinese.

Bobby Jiaolong kicked him. The man blinked and looked up at him with a tired indifference. "Hey, O'Shae, this man thinks you're a sword fighter. He wants to hire you. He's paying with gold if you can believe it."

O'Shae didn't move.

Bobby kicked him again. "O'Shae, look, he's got bags of money and he's going to get us both out of this deathtrap. All you have to do is bring that sword of yours. He's lucky I was here because he'd convinced himself you were Chinese."

O'Shae fluttered his eyes. He looked the Lawman up and down. "Swords, huh?"

"Yes."

"How much?"

The Lawman tossed a pouch into O'Shae's lap. Bobby's eyes bulged. O'Shae held the pouch in his hand and weighed it while looking over the clustered mess of the canteen. "And what am I fighting?"

"A djinn."

"In America?" O'Shae closed his eyes and mulled over the offer. In a blur of movement, the pouch disappeared into his pocket and he was on his feet. "I'll get me sword," he said.

The Lawman and Bobby Jiaolong stood outside the foreman's office, waiting for the master swordsman. Behind them, the foreman was counting his second payment for the Irishman and two horses.

"… And that's when I got banned from Les Chat Rouge. But I could have sworn that place let you touch the girls. She liked it, even. Almost woulda married her, you know. Anyway, it was about that time I…" Bobby Jiaolong was talking. He'd been talking since they left the canteen. The Lawman did his best to stare off into the distance, but Bobby didn't much seem to mind. He was listing his plans for the money, which mostly involved whiskey and cathouses, mostly.

O'Shae appeared through the dust of the planet and sauntered over like a man still asleep. He carried with him a small kerchief full of his meagre possessions. His sword was fastened to his back, wrapped in a bamboo sheath. Without acknowledging his new compadres, he climbed onto his horse and sat there waiting.

The Lawman turned to face the foreman, whose smile would remain on his face for several days. "We'll be off then, sir. Thank you for your business."

"Oh, yeah, sure. Just remember, no refunds. Especially for Bobby there."

Off the trio rode. Behind them, above the clattering of rail work, the foreman and his friends were laughing.

They rode west for two days before O'Shae spoke another word. Bobby Jiaolong, conversely, had detailed every second of his sordid American tale at least twice. The Lawman, for the first time, regretted the oaths he was bound to.

"Now this djinn bloke," was how O'Shae broke his silence, "How did he wind up over here? I had a hell of a time getting from Limerick and I'm human."

The Lawman was relieved to discover that, for all his love of talking, Bobby knew when to be quiet. "I can't tell you, to be honest. All I know is that it's here and I've fought it once before."

"So why do you need us then?"

"I think 'us' is generous, O'Shae. I need you. In our battle, we reached an impasse. Modern weapons don't work on it, you see. We came to a stalemate. It is said that whoever can best it in combat will earn three wishes."

"Ah," said O'Shae, his psyche returning to his silent ghostliness.

Bobby chuckled. "Can't believe you thought I was a sword fighter, you colossal idiot. Bet you're wishing you relied less on stereotypes now, don'tcha?"

"Shut up," said the Lawman.

"And besides all of which, what's your name, sheriff? You know both of ours."

"My name is Lawman."

"Fuck no it ain't."

"Yes, it is! It's my name! Lawman is my name."

"And lawing is your game! Aye. I get it." Bobby tried to whistle. "Lordy did I get stuck with quite the pair, eh? And we're off to fight a djinn, of all things. I don't even know what it is. I'm kind of nervous."

"O'Shae is going to fight the djinn. You are going to wait outside."

"Outside of what exactly? It better not be a cave. I got stuck in a cave when I—"

"It's not a cave! You'll see when we get there."

"And it better not be a cabin in the woods either. Those places creep me out."

"You'll see! God!"

"Right so," smiled Bobby. A pause. "So anyway, there was this young lass I met out at…"

The ruined fort lay above them at the edge of a cliff, surrounded by a thick mist. Two of its walls had been all but destroyed by artillery fire. The grounds were littered with rusted cannons, wooden spikes, rushed barricades, foxholes, and the lost souls of a thousand soldiers. A family of ravens called down from a watchtower where three hanging skeletons swung in the breeze. The grass was charred and dead. A battle had been fought, but neither side had won. Corpses in green and grey uniforms lay one next to the other, united in their dying moments in the face of pure evil.

Even as they made their way to the fort's battered gate, they could feel the djinn's presence. Its breathing seemed to take in all the air. A weak, rhythmic pulse reverberated through the dust.

The portcullis behind the gate had been torn apart and lay strewn against the fort's courtyard. While the bodies beyond the walls told the story of a battle, those inside were corpses lost to madness. Bodies lay folded over barrels of gunpowder, others bent forward into their own blades, or sat slumped against walls and broken carts with the gun barrels in their mouths. The doorway into the djinn's lair promised far more grizzly remains.

"Right, so wait out here, you said?" Bobby said, pushing the husk of a man off some sandbags so he could sit down.

The Lawman pushed open the doors of the one intact building and entered. O'Shae drew his hungry blade and followed. Inside was illuminated by flickering balls of blue energy, stuck in time. Thirty dead men stood frozen in place, their mouths wide and eyebrows furrowed. Some still crouched behind overturned tables, others set mid-walk with their pistols aimed at invisible adversaries, a few were posed crawling on the floor. Presumably crawling. The closer the Lawman looked at the bodies on the floor, the more it looked like they were being dragged toward something, the pointy nubs of their fleshless fingers sunk into the ground.

"It's waiting in the officer's quarters," the Lawman whispered.

"If you couldn't best it, how come you didn't end up like these poor bastards?"

"As I said, it was a tie."

"And how did you come to that conclusion?"

"Because neither of us can die."

"Ah. But you can't fight too well either?"

"Hmph."

The corpses closest to the captain's quarters floated in mid-air. Their flesh and bones had been torn asunder and levitated away from the bodies like heavenly bodies in orbit. Chunks of broken jaw trailed away from the shattered face of a man in the uniform of a decorated hero. The ground was buried beneath an inch of ash and blood.

The Lawman pushed open the officer's door and revealed the glowing sphere of energy. It hovered above a perfect circle of dead men, all fresh kills, their flesh still warm. The djinn had been busy.

"You again," came an ethereal voice. "I thought we'd agreed."

"Yes. And so here I am. This is my champion."

The sphere flashed three times and then disappeared. "Very well," the voice said.

"Just a moment."

The officer's chambers vanished, replaced in an instant by a marble floor, stone pillars reaching up to a whirling cyclone of purple infinity. The bodies were gone. Walls replaced by a vast emptiness. White flames ran a ring around the arena, illuminating every crevice of the room. A figure materialised. Blue skin, enormous eyes, a black ponytail, golden bracelets wrapped around its thick wrists, white, sagging pants bound to his waist by a red sash. His chest was decorated in a thousand blasphemous, perverse runes from forgotten eons. He stood examining O'Shae. O'Shae returned the gaze.

"You've told this champion of yours what I am?"

The Lawman nodded.

"And you swear to remain an impartial observer?"

"We both know I am honour bound to my oaths."

"I know far more than that, old man."

The djinn circled O'Shae and lunged at the first sign of weakness. O'Shae rolled backwards and slashed the air with his blade, its very tip caressing the muscular, sacrilegious chest of the genie. The djinn smiled, appreciative of the game in play.

O'Shae and the djinn all but danced around the arena, one directing flirtatious and exploratory swings at the other, the other returning the favour. The Lawman could do nothing but slink into the shadows and watch with his fingers crossed. O'Shae connected with a weak blow, his follow up was parried, the djinn would counterattack and O'Shae would counter in kind. It was a spiral of counters all the way down. There was something to the fight that reminded the Lawman of dancing girls, the erotic pelvic mating rituals of carnivals, a rhythm that would be considered beautiful if not for the lethal weapons in play. The Lawman's eyes grew wide. Perhaps the Irishman could pull it off. Then he would get his wishes. Then he would finally…

Just as his confidence was at its peak, O'Shae fumbled. He swung his sword too hard and too high at the djinn, and the djinn was quick to duck. His blue fist swung upward as an uppercut and sent O'Shae flying backwards, his sword fell to the ground. Its clattered echoed through the expansive void.

O'Shae shook his head and tried to regather his fleeting thoughts. The djinn seemed almost remorseful as it approached him, its own blade poised and ready.

"No…" was all the Lawman could bring himself to say.

The djinn knocked O'Shae down and mounted him. It winked at the Lawman and held its blade high above the ground.

"OK, so it's too creepy out there on my lonesome and WHAT THE FUCK IS THAT!?" Bobby Jiaolong yelled as he sauntered into the room.

The djinn twisted its head to look at the invader which was all the time O'Shae needed. He slipped out from under the entity, grabbed its wrist, and drove its own blade straight down into its opened mouth. It screamed and flickered before returning to nonexistence. For a moment the room was silent, the eternal sky above grew dark, the white flames turned an imperial violet.

The Lawman squinted at Bobby, whose head was still moving at a frenetic pace as it tried to take in an impossible realm. O'Shae reclaimed his sword and held it, unsure if the fight was over.

"But seriously? I thought this was a fort?" said Bobby.

"Ah hah! Yes! Uh, yes!" the Lawman cried triumphantly. "It is just as I planned it! We have beaten you, djinn!"

The glowing orb reappeared above them. "You know what? Fine. You can have your three wishes."

The Lawman thought he'd waved off his cohorts. He strutted to the centre of the arena and looked up at the orb. "You know what I want. I want—"

"I want to be the fastest man on Earth!" said O'Shae.

"As you wish."

The Lawman held up his hands in protest. "Now hold on just a second there. These are my wishes."

"The only thing in this room who did less in this fight was the silt on my shoes. Even the bonemeal outside has more of a claim on these wishes. Unless… you're saying you broke our agreement?"

"What? No. Anyway, that's beside the point. These are my employees, so their wishes should be mine. With that said, I command you—"

"If I could have all the good luck in the world, that would be grand," said Bobby Jiaolong.

"As you—"

"Hey! What? No. He wasn't part of the deal!"

"—Wish."

Bobby put his hand on the Lawman's shoulder. He smiled like an old friend. The Lawman hated him. O'Shae flashed out of existence for a second, only to reappear beside the Lawman. He also put a hand on his shoulder. "Go on," they said.

"You can have this last wish. It's only fair," said O'Shae.

"One for each of the team," said Bobby.

"You're damned f—" the Lawman stopped himself. "Very well. Great djinn, I wish for a revolver with unlimited bullets that can kill whatever I desire."

"That's a very wordy wish."

"Oh, and a guy who wasn't even in the fight gets to say, 'all the luck in the world' and that's just fine?"

"Yes. Because he's not an asshole."

"Djinn…"

A supernatural sigh. Not just from the orb, but the fire, the swirling oblivion overhead. "Fine. As you wish."

A revolved appeared on the floor before the Lawman. He picked it up and examined it. Five chambers, each containing a different bullet, none of which he could pry out of the gun. It was weightless, well crafted, but the Lawman looked at it like a spoiled child at a bad birthday party. "And just what exactly is this?"

"What you wished for. The important this is—"

BLAM BLAM BLAM BLAM, said the revolver. The Lawman had pointed it at the orb. The orb did not move. The revolver's chambers didn't move. No casings fell out. But for ringing ears, there was no sign the gun had ever fired.

"Nice try. Each bullet serves its own purpose, and you'll have to figure that out yourself. But they'll never run out. You're welcome, by the way."

"You know why I want this? Will it kill the man I seek?"

"I thought your type killed everyone you could?"

"You know who I'm talking about. Joshua Cr—"

"Yes, yes."

"It will kill him? Fantastic."

"Huh? No, no. It won't do anything to the man of the Cross, but it will help you in your quest all the same."

"You said it could kill anything."

"Killing isn't something that applies to that… man. Anyway. Good luck out there. Bobby Jiaolong, Tucker O'Shae, you're welcome to come visit whenever you want. Lawman, I'll see you, cowboy."

"Yeah, yeah, whatever you say," the Lawman said, walking through a newly formed vortex back into the real world.

"Bye mister djinn," said Bobby.

"Let me know how being lucky works for you, OK?"

"Will do."

Outside the ruined fort, the three men stood beside their horses. O'Shae swung his blade with the speed and precision of a hummingbird. Bobby Jiaolong began rolling dice on the floor, calling the combination each time. The Lawman alone looked downtrodden as he ran his fingers across his gift. He felt an elbow in his side. Bobby was looking at him with wishful eyes.

"So where are we off to next, then, boss?"

"What do you mean? The job is done. You're free to go. Quickly and in the opposite direction, preferably."

"No can do, chief. We're going to help you kill the Cross man. Ain't that right O'Shae?"

O'Shae was juggling his sword. "Sure."

The Lawman's sour face went even sourer as he climbed into his saddle. He nodded reluctantly. He would need friends. "I guess we better head out then."

On they rode.

The End

Epilogue

A shadow dragged out across the ground as it entered Genesis. The sun was low and angry. Black birds had claimed the town and the bodies for themselves. They cawed and flapped their wings at the approaching stranger. They did not move from their perches or from the bodies on the ground.

The shadow hung over the body of Alfredo, identifiable only by his clothes, his features devoured hours earlier. It had come too late; the serpent had seen to that.

The Lawman entered the saloon and looked over the clues Joshua Cross had left for him. A new disciple. Cross was always recruiting. Always planning for the end. Always in control of the narrative. Things would change.

If Cross could recruit disciples, the Lawman would recruit an army. And then he would put a stop to him.

He took a shovel from behind the bar and dug a grave for his fallen friend. As he dug, he was overcome with a strange sense of pride. Far too often in his line of work he'd bore witness to the end of things. Cities, lives, civilisations. The death of Genesis was something else, though. A sacrificial gesture. Cross was telling him, in his own warped way, that they were nearing the end.

An end, at least. Whose and when were still mysteries. In a way, they were irrelevant. One of them was going to die.

And either suited the Lawman.

And the second man?

Coming Spring 2021, The Cursed and The Dead: Southern Gothic.

This is a work in progress. Please enjoy this sample.

- 172 -

Southern Gothic

Chapter One: Homecoming

"**W**hat you doing all the way down here on your lonesome, boy?" the old woman croaked.

Hosanna had been expecting the question. He'd been expecting it ever since she got on the train and noticed him in first class. She'd been waiting to ask until they reached Le Marais because she was a coward. Hosanna was used to it. She knew the further north they were, the more likely her question would be met with derision and scorn. In Le Marais, however, she could flirt with the very outer edge of confrontation and get away with it. Hosanna knew from experience, and so did she. If he so much as raised an eyebrow, much less his voice, he would find himself out in the bayous with cracked ribs and his bespoke suit irreparably damaged. And that was if he was lucky.

"You going to keep me company, ma'am?" he winked.

She blushed and looked down at her shoes.

The train whistle blew to announce their impending arrival. It was an odd sight entering a town on a train, because it always came with the quickest of city tours. Swamps became shacks became above ground cemeteries and tenement buildings, then all at once streets filled with three-storey mansions, galleries, hotels. For Hosanna it said everything he needs to know about city life: it was a single-celled organism, the outer wall the most important feature but often overlooked by the self-important nucleus.

Listening to the train hiss for a half mile before it came to a complete stop, Hosanna rushed to gather his briefcase. He smiled at the old lady and whispered when he was nearest to her.

"You're welcome to join me, you know." He winked again. She collapsed into her seat, skin bright red, leaving Hosanna ample room to walk out of the carriage. All those people cramped in the other carriages, and there were only three seats spoken for in the entirety of first class. He looked back at the woman to grin. One seat would remain occupied for a few minutes more.

Exiting the train was like diving into the ocean. One overwhelming sound transformed into something else entirely. Murmuring strangers, engines, echoes, panhandlers, police whistles. It was all too much. His time in Europe had spoiled him. Even the marble arches and gilded trellises looked gaudy on American soil.

He had to be careful not to leave the station too quickly. A man of his situation leaving anywhere in a hurry was a good way to get shot. Walking at a regular pace was no guarantee of safety, but he'd made it so far.

Outside the station was another type of bustle. The streets were wide and yet still crowded. The buildings toward above him. He tried not to stay still, tried not to look like he was out of place. His suit was doing enough of that on its own. Besides, he had somewhere to be. Le Château de Phillippe on the corner of Rue Delphine and Barley Street. Any local man, woman, or child, could have directed Hosanna to the building, but he did not need directions. Not that anyone on the street would believe him, but he'd been born there. In the…

No time for that. He crossed the street and ignored the feigned attempts at friendliness, the offers of a fun night out, the clumsy approaches. He ignored them successfully until he was halfway down Barley street, when a man appeared from out of a dark alley and stopped right in front of him.

"Hey there, sorry, sir!" the stranger said.

"It's fine."

"But since I've got your attention, where are you drinking tonight?"

"I'm not drinking tonight."

"Oh, but you are, I can tell. You've got the look of a drinker. If you're new around here, I could show you a good place. Live music, beautiful women, cheap booze. They fry up all sorts in the back, too."

"I'm not drinking. I've had a long day, and I'll be sleeping in my hotel room. Alone."

Hosanna walked on, but the man had found his opening and clung to his heels. "A hotel, huh? In this part of town. The Red Cat? The Minstrel?"

"Castle Phil."

The man stopped momentarily, only to stumble over his own feet as he caught back up to Hosanna. "The Chateaux? I didn't think they allowed us folk in there unless we are working."

Hosanna shrugged and looked wearily down the street. The building was there. Waiting for him. Windows glowing, white walls immaculate, signage sparked with modernity. It had changed since he had last been there. It hadn't changed at all. The building loomed like a bent cop, smug in the knowledge it was too late for anyone to turn around. If it had arms and a billy club, it would slap it against an open palm.

"I'm allowed in there," Hosanna said finally.

"How come? I got smacked in the face just for walking to close to it one time."

"I'm sure that's the only reason anyone would ever hit you in the face."

"No, it's true. I was minding my own. But you didn't answer the question. Why are they letting you in a hotel like that?"

"Because it's where my parents died."

The stranger stopped. "No," he said.

Hosanna kept walking.

"You the What boy? You're Hosana What? I thought you were dead too?"

"Not dead, just resting."

The stranger grabbed Hosanna and turned him around. His eyes were sunken, pupils dilated and swinging from side to side. "Mister What, I don't know how they got you to come back here, but you'd best turn around. Things only got worse in there after the… after what they did. Please, please, don't go back in that place."

"I've got to."

"Why?"

Hosanna dug his knuckles into the man's sides and pushed him away. He hadn't hurt another living being in seven years, eight months, eleven days, and change. A deep pit opened up in his stomach. "No more questions. Maybe I'll buy you a drink come the weekend if the offer still stands."

"You fool. You will not make it to the weekend if you go in that place."

Hosanna retrieved some coins from his pocket and sprinkled them on the floor. The stranger could only stare at him.

"I don't want your damn money, Hosana What. You're going to die in there!"

Hosanna walked on. As if walking through an invisible barrier, the stranger and those like him stopped dead. Some turned, others stooped to collect the coins. Hosanna could feel his heart hit against his chest. He had come close. Too close. The warnings were misguided, and yet it was sad to see the building still carried the ghost of its reputation.

And it was not the only ghost it carried.

Hosanna had no choice but to return to Le Château de Phillippe because his parents, his poor, loving, dead parents, they had never left. He stood on the road looking up at the attic where it had all happened. A sudden burst of vertigo ran through him, and he looked instead at the foyer doors leading into the hotel. One man in a dark suit stood waiting for him, unsure if he should hold the door for Hosanna or call the police.

Hosanna opened the door himself and stepped inside.

Many thanks for reading this book. We hope it was time well spent. The story continues in 2021. More magic and gun smoke, more cryptids and cowboys, more lost souls and bad men (and surprisingly reasonable everyone else). See you there!

As a buyer of this book, you have beaten cancel culture. Buying our books is the only way to scientifically do this. The certificate is found nearby. If you don't buy this book and/or hate it, you are censoring us and are trying to culture us.

About the Author

Avi Llio was born in extreme circumstances and as a result was not supposed to be able to read or write. At least one of these medical assertions has since been proven false. Avi has written for television and the stage and is the 2017 Bilderberg Writing Guild recipient for Most Promising Liar. In their spare time, Avi enjoys long walks, Cowboy Bebop, and trying to find a Mexican restaurant staffed by actual Mexicans.

About Ixtab Media

We are an independent publisher of fiction. Our goal is to create engaging, inclusive, easily accessible fiction in a variety of genres. As a non-profit, we strive to pay our writers and team significantly more than they would earn at a major publisher. It is our explicit intention to create a working environment so rewarding that we're copied by more mainstream companies. We take risks, reward creativity, and explore ways to tell important stories disguised as pulp paperbacks.

Our book covers are designed by independent artists from all over the world. They receive 10% of the profits.

Feel free to contact us.

More from Ixtab Media

Coming soon or available right now. Please check our website for accurate information. We aim to deliver more books on a near-monthly basis, so please check at least five times a day. Eventually we'll get to something written just for you.

<u>Beneath Eldritch Lake</u>, **David X Reiver**

In this highly experimental horror novel, Ozymandias Caduca returns to his hometown for his father's funeral. When the body goes missing and a series of unprovoked murders are committed around town, even reality itself begins to unravel. And then things get weird.

<u>Abel High's Least Wanted</u>, **Angela Fuentes**

When all the cool, attractive, adult-looking students of Abel High are eaten by an interdimensional demon, only the kids who weren't invited to the annual basketball tournament are left standing. But if the heroic kids are dead, what chance to a bunch of outsiders who actually look their age stand?

<u>Waiting for Reckoning; or, Love and the End of Everything</u>, **D.D. James**

It is the year 22 billion AD and South, the last living thing in the universe, has decided to write his memoir. Focused mainly on his millennia-spanning search for revenge and how he found love in an Edinburgh curio museum, this book is a charming, timely meditation on complacency, guilt, loneliness, love, hope, and the systemic destruction of the plant.

<u>Dane Morris: Rise and Fall of an Ubermensch; Or, An Intellectual Derp Derp</u>, **Lazarus Tooms**

Dane Morris is a bad writer. Just awful. After murdering a publisher, he becomes a celebrity and the voice of young aspiring philosophers everywhere. Is he smart enough to realise he's being manipulated? Probably not.

CHAMPION OF FREE SPEECH*

Ixtab Media awards

____

in recognition for their brave decision to buy this book and thus
prove cancel culture is dead.

____
REX HAMMERLOCK
CEO

____
MALACHI JONES
Free Speech Advisor

*Only applicable if owner of this certificate continues to buy our products and leaves glowing five star reviews on various review sites. Anything else is cancel culture.